PRAIRIE HARDBALL

Also by Alison Gordon

Fiction

The Dead Pull Hitter (1988)
Safe at Home (1990)
Night Game (1992)
Striking Out (1995)

Non-Fiction

Foul Balls: Five Years in the American League (1984)

PRAIRIE HARDBALL

A KATE HENRY MYSTERY

by Alison Gordon

M&S

Canadian Cataloguing in Publication Data

Gordon, Alison
    Prairie hardball

"A Kate Henry mystery"
ISBN 0-7710-3412-1

I. Title.

PS8563.08353P72   1997   C813'.54   C97-930204-8
PR9199.3.G66P72   1997

The publishers acknowledge the support of the Canada Council and the Ontario Arts Council for their publishing program.

Typesetting by M&S, Toronto
Printed and bound in Canada

All the events and characters in this book are fictitious. Any resemblance to persons living or dead is purely coincidental.

McClelland & Stewart Inc.
The Canadian Publishers
481 University Avenue
Toronto, Ontario
M5G 2E9

1 2 3 4 5   01 00 99 98 97

For

Ruth Anderson Gordon (1910–1996)
and
Paul Bennett, Joe Tamani, and Stan Tonoski
(Fiji, 1995)

This book couldn't have been written without the generosity of more people in Saskatchewan than I can possibly name here, who provided me with encouragement, anecdotes, suggestions, delicious meals, and comfortable beds on my travels around my adopted province. It was CBC Radio that put me in touch with many of them, and I deplore the cuts that may destroy it. In particular, I am grateful to my fellow writers Gail Bowen, Suzanne North, and Sharon Butala; to Sergeant Bob Conlon of the Battlefords Detachment of the RCMP and to Dr. Jean Roney of the RCMP Forensic Laboratory in Regina; to Eric Peterson and Barb Cram for sharing memories of Indian Head; to Jane and Dave Shury of the Saskatchewan Baseball Hall of Fame; and to a stranger, Connie Kaldor, who kept me in touch with Saskatchewan, wherever I was writing.

Thanks also go to my friends Henri Fiks and Susan Longmire, for taking me in from the cold and providing a haven in which I could write through tough times, and to my personal three musketeers, Howard Engel, Peter Robinson, and Eric Wright for their constant encouragement and support. I am always grateful to Avie Bennett, a real champion; to Doug Gibson and Kelly Hechler; to Lynn Schellenberg; and, most of all, to Ellen Seligman.

PROLOGUE

The beam from the flashlight, bright but narrowly focused, crossed the old plank floor in wide, searching sweeps. Outside, in the early Sunday morning hours of a God-fearing town, the streets were empty, the only sound the wind rustling through poplars. When the door of what had been the town's first church opened, the only witness was a star-tled orange cat, which dashed across the lawn to the safety of the bushes. A figure emerged and slipped into the shadows around the side of the building towards the back lane. Then the muffled, cautious, clunk of a truck door shutting broke the predawn silence, followed by the cough of an engine's ignition. The tail-lights blinked briefly as the pickup turned right onto 2nd Avenue, then left on 22nd Street, Battleford's main drag. After a couple of blocks the headlights came on and the driver gunned it out of town.

Several hours later, the sun began to trickle through win-dows, gently teasing the quiet neighbourhood to life. Larks and sparrows filled the air with morning song, alarm clocks rang, screen doors slammed, and dogs let out by sleepy masters barked greetings to each other, and to the day.

Inside the old church, the darkness gradually lifted to reveal baseball bats, hats, and gloves hanging on the walls. Photographs appeared out of the gloom, of proud young men with farmers' faces above baggy uniforms, with the names of small Saskatchewan towns spelled out on their chests: Kindersley, Unity, Lanigan, Climax, Outlook.

The sun picked out the dust on the old three-ring binders on the library shelves. It illuminated first the hat, then the celluloid face of a mannequin donated by a local clothing store when its last owner retired, driven out of business by chain stores at the mall. Its moulded face and body looked too effete for the Canadian Olympic team uniform it wore.

The light touched on the racks of old team jerseys, each with its provenance pinned to its sleeve, and a case full of autographed baseballs, before sliding up the plywood ramp to the old organ at the front of the church. Sitting on the bench as if waiting for the church bell to ring was a figure dressed in the perky uniform of the All-American Girls Professional Baseball League, hands poised on the keys, head bowed, as if in prayer.

Propped on the organ's rack was the sheet music for the league's theme song. A proud group of elderly women had sung it the night before at the Saskatchewan Baseball Hall of Fame induction dinner, tears in their still-bright eyes: "We're one for all, we're all for one, we're All-American."

But there were no tears in the eyes of the organist on this all-Canadian morning. In her eyes, there was nothing but death.

CHAPTER

I

The Trans-Canada Highway east of Regina is the road of all my dreams. When I was a child, it led to adventure on school trips and family holidays. In my teens, it was my doorway to what passed for bright lights and sophistication in Saskatchewan's capital city. When I was done growing up, as then I thought, it was my escape route. Now, in my middle years, it's how I find my way home.

Andy and I were on the highway in a car we had picked up at the Regina airport, one of those tin-can hatchbacks no one but rental companies ever buys. It was painted a vivid, metallic plum that was too close to purple for my taste, but it was the only one they had left. At least we wouldn't lose it in parking lots, which is what usually happens to me with rentals.

I looked out the window, my heart filling at the sight of the prairie sky. It was my first trip to Saskatchewan in the summer in ten years, since I began covering baseball. I always come home for Christmas, but from April until October, my job keeps me on the road all over the American League.

I had almost forgotten how beautiful the prairies are in August. The fields on either side of the road made a patchwork of colour, green and gold, barley and canola. The sky, a deep, clear blue, with a few cumulus clouds sketching angel shapes at the horizon and reflecting in the sloughs by the side of the road, each with its own family of half-grown ducklings. A hawk hovered overhead, watching for unwary gophers in the fields below. I could see Indian Head's grain elevators off in the distance and I felt a stirring in me, as if an electrical circuit had been completed, filling me with the strangely calm energy I never feel in the city, in the east. I turned to Andy and smiled.

"How do you like it so far?"

He shrugged.

"What's to see?" he said.

It was Andy's first trip west. A Torontonian, born and bred, he suffers from the blind indifference to the rest of Canada typical to native sons and daughters of the Centre of the Universe. He has met my parents on their trips east, but has never before come home with me. Because his ex-wife sends the kids for part of each Christmas season, he always stays in Toronto for it. I suspect that the weather reports of blizzards and forty-below also have something to do with it. I was looking forward to showing him my home town, but I was apprehensive, too. I felt as if I was baring a secret part of my soul, and was afraid he'd find it dull or corny.

4

"You're such an easterner," I said, feeling good teasing him, feeling myself change back into Kate Henry, Prairie Girl, as the kilometres spooled beneath us. "Look up. Look at the sky."

He did so, and shrugged again.

"Bunch of clouds. Big deal," he said, enjoying his role as much as I was enjoying mine. "What do you want me to do, start reciting poetry?"

I stroked the wavy greying hair at the back of his neck.

"You're blind, Andy Munro. You have the soul of a policeman."

"That's my job, ma'am. An occupational hazard of homicide work is the lack of opportunities to find poetry in the soul."

We were almost at the turnoff for Indian Head.

"Go to the left, just ahead," I said, pointing.

He signalled a turn, moving into the left lane.

"We're almost there."

Andy leaned forward, keen, in spite of his pretence, for his first look at the very small town in which I grew up.

"Now *that's* interesting," he said, craning his neck to look at the giant statue of an Indian head, in full feathered bonnet, standing guard outside the tourist office.

"They put that up when the province moved the highway south," I explained. "To attract the tourists."

"Hard to resist," Andy said. I gave him a look I hoped would be withering, even though I also found the Indian ridiculous, not to mention politically incorrect. We drove down Railway Street towards the grain elevators, then turned left again.

"Here's Grand Avenue," I said. "Downtown Indian Head."

Andy took it in, all five low-slung blocks of it.

"Downtown," he said to me, half questioning.

"That's it," I said.

Not that I couldn't see it through his eyes. Whenever I come back, I am surprised at how small and dull it seems, a cliché straight out of W. O. Mitchell. But while Andy only saw the sleepy wide main street with pickup trucks parked diagonally in front of the low-rise building, I saw a childhood's worth of memories.

Dragan's Drugs, where I bought my mother terrible perfume for her birthdays before I knew better, and where I suffered the embarrassment every woman my age remembers, buying monthly supplies in plain brown wrappers.

The *Indian Head–Wolseley News*, where I began my journalism career as the high-school stringer, filing stories about hockey games, school plays, and the annual fashion show.

The Clip & Curl salon, also known as Pinkie's, where I got my hair teased into a beehive for the grad dance, a hairdo that lives forever in the colour portrait in my parents' front hall, faded and greenish, as embarrassing to me now as the poems I wrote back then.

The Rainbow Café, the Chinese restaurant where we went after school every day to drink sodas and act out all the dramas of our teenage lives. There's at least one Chinese café in every Saskatchewan town. I had a crush on the owner's son for one long summer, feeling daring and worldly, drawn by the exoticism of his skin and eyes.

The Nite Hawk Theatre, formerly named the Gary, after the owner's son. A new world opened to me there each week, and fuelled my dreams of escape.

And finally, the turn left on Eden Street towards St. Andrew's United Church, where my father held the pulpit for seventeen years, a wonderful old brick building that anchors the corner like a rock.

My parents no longer live in the old manse, where I grew up making friends with the ghosts with whom we shared it. They were friendly ghosts. I saw them often, and was sorry when my parents had to move out, long after I'd left town.

But when they retired, they didn't go far. They bought a bungalow directly across the street from the new church hall. It was handy, they said. The new minister, until he realized that they had no plans to meddle in his work, thought it was too handy by half.

The house is small, but the yard is huge, especially compared to the postage stamps we call property in Toronto. My father loves both flowers and vegetables, and my mother keeps busy every year pickling and preserving the bounty. I could see from the heavily laden tomato and cucumber plants that it was almost time for the annual chili sauce and sweet-pickle making. I bought her a Cuisinart a few years ago to help with the slicing and dicing. It still sits in its box. No shortcuts for Mrs. Reverend Henry.

My parents must have been watching for us out the window, because they came down the walk as soon as we parked the car, with Shadrach, their silly half-shepherd, in the lead, barking hysterically. He shut up just long enough to jam his nose into Andy's crotch. Andy, his hands full of luggage, yelped.

"He's an obedience school dropout," I explained, grabbing the dog by the collar and pulling him off.

"Welcome home," my father said. I hugged and kissed him as best I could with handfuls of dog, then did the same with my mother.

"What an extraordinary vehicle," my father said. "What would you call that colour? Plum?"

"Pimp purple," I said. My mother's response was The Look I'd grown up with, equal parts disappointment and disapproval. We went up the path to the kitchen door. The front door is only for strangers. Shadrach barrelled through our legs and generally created mayhem, his toe-nails clicking on the linoleum.

"You're in the guest room," my mother said. "Hush, Shadrach! I'll put the kettle on and we'll have tea once you're settled in. Shadrach, stop that!"

"I'll show you the way," my father said, leading Andy down the hall, Shadrach following, sniffing earnestly at his bum.

"When does Sheila get here?" I asked. My sister lives on a ranch near Shaunavon, in the southwestern part of the province, with her husband, Buddy, and their two perfect children.

"She's meeting us in Battleford, with the girls. Things are too busy on the ranch for Buddy to get away."

"Oh, that's too bad."

"Well, it will give us more of a chance to visit," she said.

"Of course."

I leaned against the counter and watched her get the tea things ready. She is a tall woman, still slim, with her once-red hair, now white, parted in the middle and pulled back into a bun at the back of her head, the curls we share under strict control. She wore a flower-print housedress, with an apron over it. She always wears dresses. I don't think I've seen her in pants, except when she's at the cabin in the summer.

She made the tea in the "good" teapot, the one that had belonged to her mother, and set out the dainty porcelain teacups that I thought so beautiful when I was a child. They are all different floral patterns, made of china so thin you can see through it.

After a few awkward minutes of conversation, I excused myself to help Andy unpack, and found him in the guest room, gawking in horror at the twin beds, each with its ruffled comforter. Little-girl beds.

"I'm surprised they didn't put us in separate rooms."

"They would have if they had the space," I whispered back, then closed the door.

"Can we push them together?"

"Not on your life. You don't think I would actually *do it* in my parents' house, do you?"

"Why not?"

"I couldn't."

"You're forty-five years old, Kate."

"Not in this house, I'm not."

I undid our garment bag, pulled out the things on hangers and hung them in the closet.

"Besides, the beds squeak," I said.

"You know this from experience?" he asked, unzipping his pants.

"What are you doing?"

"Relax. I'm just changing into jeans."

I grabbed him and gave him a quick squeeze, then left the room. When I got back to the kitchen, the kettle had just begun to whistle.

"Where's Andy, dear?"

"He's just getting changed."

"He's all right now, is he?" she asked. Andy had been wounded in a shooting last summer. It had been a long and sometimes difficult recovery.

"He's fine. I told you about his promotion, didn't I?"

"Yes, Inspector Munro. He must be pleased."

"I'm not sure. He's a supervisor now. I think he's frustrated being out of the action. I know he hates the paperwork. On the other hand, there's not as much danger riding a desk, which makes me happy. Is there anything I can do to help?"

"Just take the tray in to Dad. I'll bring the cookies."

My father was sitting in the living room in his favourite chair. He smiled wearily when I came in, and I was struck by how frail he looked. He's almost eighty now, and he has aged an alarming amount in the last few years. I think his arthritis gives him more pain than he admits to.

"It's good to see you, Daddy," I said.

"It's nice to have you home. Your mother misses you."

I put the tray down on the coffee table.

"Me too," I said, and wished I could say more. But it's not something we go in for much in the Henry family. In the rest of my life I have no problem with talking about things that matter, but get me back in my parents' living room, and the old Presbyterian genes take right over. No fuss, no regrets.

I faintly envy my friends who are close with their parents, who confide in them every little thing, but I think at heart I'd rather keep my secrets. There's something a little unseemly about having a parent as a pal.

10

CHAPTER

2

True to her Supermum form, my mother had baked my favourite chocolate-chip cookies for my homecoming, which she brought into the living room and put next to the tea tray.

She was the reason I had begged off the first half of a two-week Titan home stand to make the trip. Back in the forties, before she met my father, Helen MacLaren, as she then was, had been one of fifty-odd Canadians to play in the All-American Girls Professional Baseball League, the one celebrated in the movie *A League of Their Own*. Half of them came from Saskatchewan, and those "girls," Mum included, were to be inducted into the Saskatchewan Baseball Hall of Fame in Battleford on the weekend.

My mother and I have never been close. I was a dreamy sort of child, and she admired practicality. I was sloppy and forgetful (still am) and she thought tidiness next to godliness. As a teen, I found her smug conventionality stifling and was unable to comprehend her contentment with a life revolving around parish work, the hospital board, and weekly visits to the salon.

My father, a scholar and a dreamer in his own way, was my hero. He had travelled as a young man. He had gone to University of Toronto. He had visited London and Paris, Rome and Florence. He had served as a chaplain in World War Two. When I was still little, my best treat was to spend Friday evenings curled up in the armchair in his study reading while he worked on his sermon.

My only bond with my mother was forged on Saturday afternoons. It was she who taught me to love baseball. I couldn't meet her standards on the field, but she did manage to teach me how to throw hard, not like a girl, a skill that gives me credibility at the ballpark even now.

More importantly, she taught me to watch, to understand strategy, to think like a ballplayer. She had been a backup outfielder for the Racine Belles, and had used her time on the bench well. As in major-league baseball, it is not necessarily the biggest stars who best understand the game. To this day, when I want fresh insight, I go to the utility players in the clubhouse, not the multi-million-dollar guys.

Indian Head was a baseball town, host to fierce annual provincial tournaments in the fifties. For a few seasons, the Indian Head team was all black, recruited from the southern United States to give us a lock on all the tournaments. I can't imagine what those players must have made of lily-white rural Saskatchewan back then.

When there was no game in town, we would find one on the radio or, later, on television. My mother being my mother, she would peel vegetables or do her mending in front of the set, but she never missed an inning. She was more passionate about the game of baseball than she seemed to be about anything else in her life. I know that the only times I ever heard her raise her voice was to argue an umpire's call.

She still follows the game, especially the team I cover, the Titans. When I phone home each week, she can be counted upon to second-guess the manager's moves. I once passed on one of her suggestions to Sugar Jenkins, the hitting coach, and it's become a running gag in the clubhouse to ask me what my mother would have done.

"Mum, do you still have that scrapbook I used to look at when I was a kid?" I asked her, after she finished pouring. "I bet Andy would like to see it."

"Oh, he probably doesn't want to be bothered," she said.

"Of course I do," Andy said.

"Well, I did have to get it out anyway, for the dinner. The Hall of Fame people asked me to bring it."

"I'll fetch it," my father said, getting out of his chair.

"Wait until you see her in uniform," I told Andy.

"Like in that movie you took me to?"

"Exactly," I said. "Mum looks just like Geena Davis."

"Hardly, dear," she said.

"Did you see the movie, Helen?" Andy asked.

"Yes. Some of it was quite good."

"But it was really like that? You really had charm school and chaperones and all of that?"

"Of course. My parents would never have let me go if it wasn't for the chaperones. I was only twenty, after all."

"And Racine, Wisconsin was Sodom and Gomorrah rolled into one," I laughed.

"Compared to Wolseley, Saskatchewan, it was," my father said, limping back into the room, favouring his bad hip.

"Did you ever see her play?" Andy asked him.

"Just once. When I went to Racine to ask her to marry me."

"And you accepted on the spot?" Andy asked my mother.

"Of course not," she said, almost smiling. "I waited until the season was over."

"Baseball came first in those days," Dad said, handing Andy the big blue album, held together with laces. I went and sat beside him on the couch while he opened it and turned the thick pages to the first picture.

"I remember this one," I said. "It was my favourite."

I pointed at the clipping from the Regina *Leader-Post* in 1946 which showed my mother sliding into second base, skirt flying, just ahead of the tag. Her hat had blown off and her curls were wild against her cheek.

"It's not very ladylike," she said, sitting next to Andy on the other side of the couch.

"I don't imagine ladylike probably cut it on the ball diamond, even in those days," I said.

"I remember that game like it was yesterday. Edna Adams hit a home run in the bottom of the ninth and we beat the Rockford Peaches for the championship."

"Is she going to be at the ceremony? Edna Adams?"

"I hope so. I've lost touch with most of the girls, but the last I heard, she was living in Watrous. She's widowed, I think. Edna Summers, she is now."

"What about Virna Wilton?" I asked. "She was a good friend, wasn't she?"

14

"She's coming up from Indiana, with her son. I got a letter just last week."

"Any other team-mates?"

"I think there are five of us still alive from the Belles. Five from Saskatchewan, that is. I don't know about the American girls."

"And they're all going to be there?"

"Far as I know."

"How many are going to be inducted?" Andy asked.

"Twenty, if they all come," my Dad said.

"You must be very excited," Andy said.

"It was a long time ago," she said, turning the pages of the album. "We probably won't have anything to say to each other."

That's Mum. She's spent her life protecting herself against disappointment. Of course, she has also protected herself from spontaneity or surprise, but she's willing to make the trade-off.

The clock on the mantel in the hall whirred, hiccuped, and gave four feeble dings. My mother closed the book and got up.

"I'd better be seeing to supper," she said.

"Can I help?" I asked, knowing the answer.

"No, you just relax. You've had a long trip."

"I think I've got enough energy left to peel a potato or two," I said.

"You stay and talk to your father," she said, firmly, and left the room.

He smiled.

"She's the boss."

"So, Daddy, what's new?" I asked.

"Nothing much," he said. "The usual."

"Is your hip bothering you? I notice you're limping a bit."

He waved his hand dismissively.

"Just getting a bit creaky," he said.

"You should have it replaced," I said. "Andy's step-father had it, and he's walking really well now."

"It's not so bad I can't handle it."

Silence fell in the room. Shadrach got up from the floor where he had been lying and started to climb up onto to the armchair I had been sitting in.

"Oh, dear, I'd better get his blanket or your mother will have a conniption."

"I'll get it," I said. "Where is it?"

"In the hall closet. She wanted things to be nice for you."

"Treating us like company, eh? I don't know whether to be insulted or flattered."

I covered the armchair with Shadrach's red plaid blanket. He climbed on and curled up in a ball, letting out little grunts of pleasure, gazing adoringly at my father. My family has always had dogs, but I moved on to cats the moment I left home. My current one is Elwy, who is getting on in cat years. He's probably lived about eight and a half of his lives by now, and is fairly obnoxious in his dotage. But he doesn't stick his nose into people's crotches or bark. And I don't have to follow him down the street at seven o'clock in the morning in the dead of winter, carrying a plastic baggy.

"Your mother is more excited about this trip than she's letting on," Daddy said.

"I know that."

"We'll drive to Saskatoon tomorrow and stay over with Merle and Stanley."

My father's sister and brother-in-law. We had been over these plans several times by phone over the past months.

"Are they coming to Battleford, too?"

"No, he's not up to it, after his surgery."

"You know, Daddy, Andy and I could stay in a hotel in Saskatoon. It will be less trouble for them."

"Merle wouldn't hear of it," he said. "They've got room."

"It just seems like a lot of trouble."

"It's no trouble. They're family."

It wasn't worth fighting.

"I wish you had let us meet you at the airport. It's a shame for you to go to all the expense of renting a car when we could have all driven up together in the Chrysler."

We'd been through this before, too.

"We both like driving, Daddy. Besides, this way it gives us more flexibility if we want to do different things."

In fact, it had been a condition of Andy's agreeing to come.

"If you're sure," my father said. "But we'd like to pay for the gas."

"Daddy, you are on fixed income. Andy and I both have jobs. We can afford the gas. We don't feel put out in any way. We made the decision to take this trip, and we're delighted we did. Aren't we, Andy?"

"Of course," he said. "I've always wanted a chance to dig up all the secrets in Kate's past."

CHAPTER

3

Andy handled supper admirably. I'm sure my parents didn't notice his distress. It was a typical prairie supper: ham with new potatoes, peas, and a salad, all fresh from the garden, three kinds of homemade pickles, home-baked bread, and, of course, a Saskatoon-berry pie. With second helpings encouraged. The sheer volume was enough to nonplus him, but the timing threw him completely. In typical prairie fashion, we were finished, with the dishes done, by six o'clock, an hour before we even contemplate dinner in Toronto. We left my parents listening to the CBC news and went for a walk.

I revert quickly when I come home to the different pace of life. So I found myself struggling to keep up with his impatient Toronto stride.

"Hold up," I said, "or else we'll have seen the whole town before I've finished my smoke."

He didn't know what I was talking about.

"Slow down, Andy, you're in Saskatchewan now. You don't have to rush. No one's going to get there before you."

"There's no there to get to anyway," he grumbled.

I took his arm, partly for companionship and partly to hold him back. It was a beautiful evening. The sun was getting low in the sky, and the light was so soft and luminous I could almost feel it caressing my skin. It felt like home.

I worried about Andy on this trip. Even though I got out of Indian Head as fast and as far as I could once I had the chance, it's still part of who I am. As are my parents. I couldn't expect him to embrace my world, but I wanted him to see what was good about it. Being with him here made me a little edgy, as if my home town was on trial.

The streets were emptier than when I was a child playing after supper. I suppose the current generation is more interested in Nintendo than kick-the-can, although we did see some boys on bicycles, riding no-hands.

"I wonder where they're going," Andy said.

"Boy business," I said. "When I was a kid, I always wanted to go with them on their adventures. They seemed to have more fun than the girls."

"I can't imagine that ever stopping you."

"I wonder if they still play cowboys and Indians. That was big when I was a kid. That and war. There's probably some politically correct alternative now."

"What did girls play?"

"House, and brides, and being members of the Royal Family. Except when I went to my friend Doreen's. She lived on a farm."

"What would you play then, farm chores? Milk maids?"

"Her dad had a couple of old workhorses we'd ride bareback and be Indian warrior maidens."

"Warrior maidens?"

"Yeah. The only problem was, we had to walk the horses across the pasture first, then get on and they would walk back to the barn. Slowly. It was good enough at the time, though."

A dog barked from the porch of a big brown stucco house with the front yard full of caragana bushes.

"That's where my friend Gail lived," I said. "Her dad worked at the forestry farm. She collected bugs, which made her very popular with the boys. The other girls thought she was gross, but I liked her a lot."

"You know what surprises me?" Andy asked. "There are so many trees. I thought that Saskatchewan didn't have any trees."

"Another myth perpetrated by Eastern bastards. The Saskatchewan motto should be 'Every tree a wanted tree.' And almost all of them came from the forestry farm outside town. That big old spruce tree in Gail's backyard was the first conifer west of the Rockies, or so her dad used to tell us."

"It's prettier than I thought."

"It's beautiful here. That's what I've always told you."

"Okay, so I didn't believe you. Sue me."

We walked on for a while in silence, past the community skating rink.

"Lots of memories there?" he asked.

"Oh, yeah. Well, at the old rink, anyway. It was a wonderful place. The wood floors were all scarred from our skate blades, and there was a stove to keep us warm. The first time I ever held hands with a boy was there, when I was about twelve. Bobby LaPointe. He was the RCMP constable's son. He wasn't afraid of me because I was the preacher's daughter. I think he was actually a Catholic. He was older, too, like about fourteen. We skated with our mittens off, which was a very big deal."

"Major prairie rite of passage, I guess," Andy snickered, taking my hand.

"Oh, yeah, Mr. Sophistication. What was yours?"

"Spin the bottle in the basement rec room, probably."

"Oh, very worldly."

"But when we got older, we could go to Yonge Street on the subway with false ID and hang around Le Coq D'or listening to Ronnie Hawkins. Or to Yorkville to smoke dope. Where did you go?"

"The nuisance grounds."

"The what grounds?"

"The dump. That's where we went to drink and make out."

"Charming."

"Well, it had one advantage. You could see the cops coming from a long way away. By the time they got there, our beer bottles would be indistinguishable from the rest of the garbage."

"This explains a lot."

"Like what?"

"Well, since your happiest teenaged memories were at the dump, I can understand why your study is the way it is."

When we got to the corner of Howard Street, I stopped.

21

"Okay, we're here," I said. "Look around you. This is an important landmark of my youth."

He did a 360-degree turn, looking around the neighbourhood of newish houses for something that could possibly be of interest. I could see by his expression that he had failed.

"When I was a teenager," I said, "this was the edge of town. From here on, it was bald prairie. I used to stand here and tell myself I was in the Middle of Nowhere. That's with capital letters."

"You weren't far from right."

"And then I would tell myself that I was going to go capital-S Somewhere and be capital-S Somebody."

"And?"

"I guess I have. It doesn't feel the way I thought it would, somehow."

He put his arms around me.

"You're somebody in my books," he said.

"Thanks," I said, hugging him back. "Still, sometimes I wonder what I would be like if I had stayed."

"A fate too horrible to contemplate."

I disentangled myself.

"I don't know," I said. "Who knows what I could have made of myself here?"

"You could have been keeper of the Indian Head statue."

"Exactly," I said. We headed back towards Grand Avenue.

"Does everybody here drive a pickup truck?" Andy asked, as another one drove by, slowing to check us out.

"Lots of them do. Farmers and ranchers need them for their work. The rest, I guess, just like trucks."

"I like trucks, too. Why don't we get one?"

"Right. A pickup truck in Toronto."

"Why not? It would be great for hauling things."

"Hauling things."

"Like when we buy antiques in the country."

"Which we have done exactly once in our collective life."

"We could do it more, if we had a truck."

"And where would we find room for these famous antiques? Our place is already full."

"Well, maybe not antiques then, but stuff."

"And where would we park this pickup truck?"

"In the garage."

"And our cars?"

"We could sell yours."

"Oh, now it's me driving the pickup truck around downtown Toronto. Forget it."

"It would be safer than your Citroën. Sitting up high, you could see right over the traffic."

"Your concern for my safety is touching," I said. "But if you want a truck, you'll be driving it."

"Spoilsport."

"That's me. No fun at all. Speaking of which, we've pretty much wrapped up the trip down memory lane," I said. "What do you want to do? Do you want to go to the Rainbow Café for a coffee?"

"What about a drink? Haven't had one of those in a while."

"I guess we could go to the beer parlour," I said.

"The nightlife hot spot, no doubt."

"That and the Legion Hall. But you've got to be a member."

We walked up to the Sportsman's Bar, which had replaced the old hotel when it burned down a few Christmases ago. I paused outside the frosted-glass doors.

"It's not very grand," I said.

"I can take it, trust me."

I was surprised when we walked in. The carpeting on the floor was clean, and the Formica tables were new. The place was nearly full, with a lot of action around the small pool table and a row of video gambling machines, where skinny men in jeans and baseball caps pumped in coins, squinting through their cigarette smoke at electronic fruit lined up losers. The television sets were turned to the ball game back in Toronto. We found a table and sat down.

"I guess a fine single-malt is out of the question," Andy said.

"A martini would be dicey, too," I agreed, "and I wouldn't ask for the wine list."

The waitress came to the table.

"Hey, Kate, how are you?"

I looked up. Hidden behind the makeup and country-and-western hairdo was a face I knew. I searched the dustier corners of my brain for the name.

"Doreen, it's great to see you," I said, and meant it. I turned to Andy.

"Doreen was my best friend back in school," I explained. "I was just telling you about her."

"The one with the horses," Andy said, shaking her hand.

"Right, remember when we would play warrior maidens?"

24

"Among other things too embarrassing to talk about," she laughed, hip cocked against an empty chair.

"So, catch me up," I said. "What's your news?"

"Ed and I divorced a while back. You probably heard. The kids are all grown. I'm even a grandma, if you can believe that."

"No, I can't, Doreen. That's incredible. I was sorry about the divorce, though."

"Ancient history," she shrugged. "What can I get you?"

I ordered a vodka and tonic. Andy asked for Scotch.

"Coming right up."

"When you're not busy, come back and talk," I said, then after she left, turned to Andy. "That's sad, her ending up here."

"Don't be a snob," Andy said. "How do you know it's not exactly what she wants?"

"Not Doreen. When we were in high school we both dreamed about getting out of this place. She even had a scholarship to the university in Saskatoon. But she never made it."

"How come?"

"The typical story of women of my generation. She got pregnant, married, and tied down to the farm. Her daughter followed in her footsteps, from the sound of it. She's my age and she's a grandmother already."

"There but for the grace of God?"

"You've got it."

I looked around the room. The crowd was mixed, young and old, mainly male. I looked at the middle-aged ones, trying to see if I knew any of them. At a table of business types, one of them caught my eye and raised his beer glass. There but for the grace of God, indeed. It was

Oren Roblin, my first serious boyfriend. He and I had spent a lot of time at the nuisance grounds and parked on some of the lonelier grid roads around town the summer before I left home. His uncle owned the drugstore, and he could get all the condoms he wanted, so I had avoided Doreen's fate.

I hadn't spoken to Oren in years. I had followed him through the pages of the *Indian Head–Wolseley News*, the weekly paper. My parents subscribe for me. He's a big cheese now. Chamber of Commerce. Homecoming Committee. He's even had a stint as mayor.

He spoke to the other men at his table and got up. As he moved towards us, I could see that the years had played their tricks on him. He had lost the easy grace of his teen years and his chiselled good looks had got lost in jowls. When we were young, he had a wild mane of curly hair. Now, with it cut short at the sides and receding at the temples, he bore an alarming resemblance to John Diefenbaker in his middle years. But the eyes were the same, those blue, blue eyes that still appear in my dreams from time to surprising time.

"How are you, Oren?" I looked up at him and put out my hand.

"Long time no see," he said, taking it gently in his big palm and looking into my eyes. I broke contact first.

"Andy, this is Oren Roblin, an old friend," I said, trying to keep my voice neutral. "Oren, Andy Munro, from Toronto."

Oren let go of my hand and grasped Andy's.

"Why don't you join us?" Andy asked, mischief in his eyes. He hadn't missed a nuance.

"Don't mind if I do," Oren said, pulling out a chair. Doreen appeared immediately with our drinks.

"Same again, Oren?" she asked.

"Sure, why not?"

She put our drinks down, winking at me.

"Old times, eh, Kate?"

I just shook my head and laughed. Doreen leaned closer.

"Your guy's a hunk," she whispered.

"I'm not sure hunks are allowed to be forty-five."

"Middle-aged hunks are the best. And he's definitely a middle-aged hunk."

She went back to work. I turned back to my middle-aged hunk and my old flame and waited for the fun to begin.

CHAPTER

4

My father was waiting up when we rolled in at about eleven, well past his bedtime, just in case we needed anything, he said. Like an extra dose of guilt. Andy and I slept badly in our chaste little beds, waking up several times in the night to grumble at each other. I gave up trying just before 7:00, and got up to make coffee. My mother had beat me to it. Dressed in her best flowered housecoat, she was already setting the table for breakfast.

I poured myself a coffee and sat down at the table, yawning, my head throbbing a bit from the excesses of the night before. Shadrach lay at my feet and sighed. It was too early for him, too.

"I'm surprised to see you up at this hour," she said.

"It's such a beautiful day, I couldn't resist," I lied.

"We have a long drive ahead of us. We'd best get an early start," she said, crisply, opening the refrigerator.

"How do you want to go? I thought Andy and I might drive up to the lake on the way."

"You know your father likes the direct route, through Regina."

She took out eggs, bacon, sausages, and butter, then got a mixing bowl down from the cupboard.

"We'll have pancakes for breakfast," she said. "Does Andy like pancakes?"

"We don't usually have time for breakfast. Pancakes would be great. But for the drive, we don't have to go in convoy, do we? I'd like Andy to see Katepwa Beach. I thought we could stop and have a swim."

"Your father likes to stop at Davidson for lunch."

"We could go north from Fort Qu'Appelle and take the Yellowhead for a change."

"You can ask him yourself then."

"I will."

I poured myself another cup of coffee and craved the *Globe and Mail*. I never feel like my day has begun until I do the cryptic crossword. Besides, I could have hidden my bad mood behind it.

"I guess you made quite a night of it," my mother said, after a few minutes. She was stirring the pancake batter.

"Not really. We just stopped in at the Sportsman's for a few drinks. It was hardly a debauch. We ran into some old friends and got talking."

"Who did you see?"

"Her old boyfriend Oren, for one," Andy said, coming into the room, dressed in jeans and a tee-shirt, his feet bare, his hair sticking out in all directions, and with a greying stubble on his cheeks. He yawned hugely without covering his mouth, which earned him a disapproving glance from my mother that he missed. I didn't. I got up to get him a cup of coffee.

"Oren Roblin has done very well for himself," my mother said, pointedly.

"I don't know about that," I said. "You'd think he'd have something better to do than hang around the beer parlour."

I got up and got a frying pan out of the cupboard, determined to be of some help.

"I'll start the sausages."

"Oh, all right," she said. "But use the cast-iron pan. I'm using that pan for the pancakes."

We worked together, side by side.

"You can't blame Oren," she said, after a few minutes. "Since his children left home, I expect he's been a bit lonely."

"What about his wife? What about Julie?"

His wife. My mother looked uncomfortable.

"She passed on several years ago, didn't you know?"

"I must have missed it in the *News*," I said. "How did she die?"

"I don't like to speak ill of the dead," she said.

"Who aren't you speaking ill of now, Helen?" my father asked, coming into the kitchen. He was already showered, shaved, and fully dressed. Shadrach struggled to his feet to offer his master a morning greeting. Then he went to the door and scratched on it. My father let him out.

"Poor Julie Roblin," my mother said, handing him his prune juice.

"Oh, that was quite the scandal," my father said.

"A scandal? Julie Roblin?" I asked.

"I'm afraid she took her own life, poor thing," my father said.

"Why?"

My mother looked uncomfortable.

"She was evidently, well, involved with someone other than Oren," she said. "Their cars were seen parked together out on the grid road behind the Orange Home and some busybody brought the news directly to coffee row. She gassed herself with carbon monoxide in her car rather than face the music. It destroyed poor Oren. Simply destroyed him. He was mayor at the time."

"Who was the other man?"

"It was Ed Wade, who had the farm out towards Sintaluta."

"Holy smokes," I said, then explained to Andy. "Ed Wade was Doreen's husband."

"They divorced shortly afterwards," my mother said. "I'm afraid he took to drink."

"That's not all he took to," my father said. "He also took it to Doreen, if you know what I mean."

"He abused her?" I asked.

"Not for long," my father said drily. "Your friend kicked him out pretty smartly."

"Well, at least she got that right," I said. "She mentioned last night that she had divorced, but she didn't say why."

"It's not the kind of thing you mention casually in a bar, Kate," Andy pointed out.

"I guess not. Anyway, that's horrible. For both of them."

"Well, it certainly kept the town talking," my father said.

"Some of the town," my mother said, primly.

"Kate's mother doesn't approve of gossip," Daddy told Andy.

"Look what it drove that poor woman to," she said.

Much as I dislike agreeing with my mother, her point was well taken. In small towns the narrowest minds create community standards, and God help the poor souls who don't conform.

"Well, I guess you're right on that one, dear, but most of it is harmless," he protested.

"If you call destroying reputations harmless, you're a lesser man than I thought you were," she countered.

"This is a never-ending battle," I explained to Andy.

"Your father has become worse since he retired," she said. "Since he became a regular on coffee row."

"Coffee row?" Andy asked.

"A bunch of old fools who have nothing better to do than go to the café every morning and jaw," she said.

"The heart and soul of the community," my father corrected.

"Not to mention the eyes and ears, and judge and jury," I said. "Every small town in Saskatchewan has at least one."

"They mind everybody's business but their own," my mother added. By unspoken agreement, we all let it be the last word.

After breakfast, my mother went to change, leaving the dishes for Andy and me. My father took Shadrach for a walk down to the post office. When he came back, he had mail in his hand.

"Letter for you, Helen," he said. "No return address. Must be a secret admirer."

"Just put it on the kitchen table," she called from the living room.

"The rest are just bills," he said. "Bills, bills, bills."

He wandered out of the room shuffling through them, Shadrach trailing behind. My mother picked up her letter.

"My glasses," she said. "Where did I put my glasses?"

"You need one of those things around your neck," I said, putting the last of the saucers away. "Sit down, I'll go look."

I found them on the table beside her chair in the living room. She opened the letter and drew out a sheet of ruled paper.

"Oh, my," she said, when she had read it.

"What is it?" I asked.

"See for yourself."

I recognized the handwriting. Not personally, but I know the style from crank mail I get at work. It was written in a tight, angry script. The different colours of ink used for underlining were another clue. Not to mention the exclamation points.

STAY AWAY from Battleford, if you know what's good for you! Women like you don't deserve to be in the HALL OF FAME!! This great institution must not be SULLIED with the likes of YOU!! No unnatural women allowed!! JUST STAY AWAY. This is NOT a joke!!!

The last line was in a particularly lurid Day-Glo lime green.

33

"Charming," I said, handing the note to Andy. "Another testosterone junkie who thinks baseball's a boys-only game."

"Well, he's certainly hostile," my mother said, looking uncomfortable.

"I wouldn't worry about it, Mum."

"She's right, Helen," Andy said. "People who write letters like these seldom do anything more."

"Really, we get them all the time at the paper," I said. "They scare you at first, but they're not serious."

"What isn't serious?" my father asked, coming into the room.

We showed him.

"For heaven's sake! What is this nonsense?" He looked at us all, alarmed, then took my mother's hand and patted it.

"Don't fret, old girl. Remember, you've got your own personal policeman along."

"That's right," I laughed. "Andy will keep you safe."

"Don't be silly," she said, briskly. "I don't need a body-guard. This is just some crackpot. Let's get going."

After a round of bathroom stops, Daddy took Shadrach and his dinner bowl down the street to the neighbour who was looking after him, while Andy packed the bags in the cars. My parents had two big suit-cases for the four-day trip. Andy and I had everything we needed for a week in a garment bag and a carry-on.

My mother did one last circuit of the house to make sure everything was in order.

"Got your glasses?"

"In my purse." She patted her white straw bag in confirmation.

"And you're not worried about that letter?" I asked.

"Don't be silly, of course not," she said, going to the hall closet for her raincoat. "It's not the first one as a matter of fact. Another came last month."

"From the same guy?"

"Could be."

"Do you still have it?"

"No, I put it in the trash, where it belonged. It was just a copy of an article from the Battleford newspaper about the awards, and he had written rude things in the margins in that same green ink."

"Did you show it to anyone? Daddy?"

"I didn't want to worry him." She took the house keys from the hook by the door.

"Ready to go?"

I picked up the letter from the kitchen table.

"I'm taking this along."

"If you must. I don't want to make a fuss."

"Maybe we should talk to the police in Battleford, too. I'll see what Andy thinks."

"Let's get going. Mustn't keep the men waiting."

She locked the door, then tried the handle.

"Better safe than sorry!"

"Exactly. And that's why we'll tell the Battleford police."

"A lot of fuss over nothing," she said.

CHAPTER

5

The River View Inn, the official hotel of the Saskatchewan Baseball Hall of Fame, was a charmless four-storey brick building just past the Battleford turnoff on Highway 16, with nary a river in sight. A "No Vacancy" sign flickered feebly through the soggy gloom, under a larger sign welcoming Hall of Fame inductees.

It had rained all the way from Saskatoon, an hour and a half through a heavy, nasty downpour that the windshield wipers could barely control. Andy was driving, and he was not happy. My aunt and uncle are sweet, but, to be absolutely honest, not the most scintillating couple in the world. And Auntie Merle, hard as she tries, will never measure up to my mother in the kitchen. Dinner had been grey roast beef with canned gravy, accompanied by mushy carrots and watery, undercooked scalloped potatoes. The conversation had centred around their most recent trip to see their grandchildren in

Kamloops, including reports on the state of all the high-ways along the way. Uncle Stan had approved of the route we had taken from Indian Head – my father's route through Davidson, of course. Actually, the lunch stop in Davidson had turned out to be the high point of the trip for me. I had found a surprise for Andy in the washroom, which had a novelty condom machine. I chose a Nite-Glow because I couldn't resist the sales pitch: "Turn out the lights and watch the glow grow and grow." Of course, at my uncle and aunt's we slept in bunk beds. And they didn't let me smoke in the house.

"Here we are," Andy said, docking in front of the main door. "Home sweet home away from home."

"It can only get better from here on," I said.

"Listening to a bunch of old biddies talking baseball is certainly my idea of a dream vacation."

I sighed and got out of the car. Andy popped the trunk lock and I got the bags out.

"I'll go park the car," he said.

"I can do it if you don't want to get wet."

"I'll get wet anyway, helping your parents with their eighty-seven suitcases."

I slammed the door, then slapped a smile on my face for my parents, who were just pulling in. I opened the door to let my mother out, then leaned in to speak to my father.

"Andy will help you with the bags in a second," I said. "Mum and I will check in."

The lobby was small, clean, and functional, with racks of tourist brochures and a soft-drink machine. A sign by the entrance to the bar, called Shooters, promised "Happy Hour Nitely, 4–6." Whoopee. The youngish woman in charge wore a bright green vest and a Hall of Fame baseball cap.

"Welcome to the River View Inn," she said cheerfully. "I sure hope you have a reservation, because we're all filled up."

We assured her that we did, and she passed cards across the counter for us to fill out.

While I was printing our particulars, Andy struggled through the double glass doors with the bags, drenched. I bit my lip to stifle the laugh that would have been suicidal under the circumstances.

"I've got nice adjoining rooms for you on the fourth floor," the clerk said. "That's in non-smoking."

And spelled double trouble. I saw the out and grabbed it.

"That must be the room for Sheila and the girls," I said to my mother. "You'll want the grandchildren next door." Not to mention poor Andy had maxed out on Henry family togetherness. We ended up on the third floor.

We had to walk past the hotel pool to get to the elevator. There were potted palms and beach umbrellas scattered around it in an apparent attempt to make the patrons feel as if they were at a resort in some salubrious southern clime. The area echoed with the splashes of children using a water slide which spiralled down from the ceiling two storeys above and there was an unmistakable whiff of chlorine, a drawback, I would have thought, for patrons of the poolside restaurant. Nonetheless, there was a large and cheerful group at several tables pushed together. Most of them were older women.

"Mum, look, those must be your friends."

She looked at them, nervously.

"Aren't you going to say hello?"

"I'll just freshen up first," she said.

They didn't give her a chance. A woman wearing a mauve pants suit got up from the table and bustled over to us, pushing a bright blue wheeled walker in front of her. Everything about her was round, her tightly curled grey hair, her pink cheeks, her merry eyes, her body. She was instantly likeable.

"Helen? Helen Henry, it *is* you, isn't it?"

My mother smiled.

"Edna Summers, you haven't changed a bit."

"A bit broader in the beam," she said, "and the knees are shot, but with this contraption I'm frisky as ever."

Then Edna, she of the famous championship-winning home run against the Rockford Peaches, hustled my mother over to the group at the table.

"Look who's here! Wheels MacLaren!"

Wheels? We followed them to the table, where my mother was the flustered, but beaming, centre of attention. While we were being introduced to all of the women and their friends and relations, I was struck by their wonderful variety. Some, like Edna, resembled the small-town women I had grown up with. Others were more sophisticated. They were tall, short, fat, thin; dressed in linen, in polyester, in dresses, in pants; hair permed, hair bobbed, grey, blue, blonde, bottle-black. They looked like grannies, they looked like librarians, they looked like gym teachers, dog groomers, duchesses, Hungarian madames. I couldn't keep track of their names.

My parents sat down at the table. Andy and I took their bags to their room, then went to ours. It wasn't the kind of four-star accommodation I was used to while travelling with the ball team, but what it lacked in terry-cloth robes and bath oils it made up for in privacy. And it had a king-sized bed.

I lit a smoke and went to the window and cranked it open. Beyond the parking lot and highway, I could see the North Saskatchewan River valley, and if I pressed my cheek against the glass, a sliver of what might just be water.

"Look," I said. "The river view."

While Andy changed into dry clothes, I checked the phone book. We stopped by the poolside table on the way back out.

"We've got an errand to run," I told my father, giving him his room key.

"We have to be at the lunch at noon," he fussed.

"We'll be back in plenty of time."

With the map of The Battlefords Andy had picked up at the front desk, it wasn't hard to find what we were looking for: a sign with the stylized sheaf of wheat used to identify government buildings.

"Bingo," I said, parking outside.

The Liquor Board store gave Andy something new to scoff at while we hunted for the single-malt Scotch.

"I've never seen so many different kinds of rye," he said, in amazement. "There are acres of rye in here."

"This is nothing," I said. "I once counted thirty-seven brands in the big store in Regina."

The Scotch was hidden in a corner next to the brandies and other exotic libations, and we managed to find the Glenlivet.

"The weekend just looked up," he said.

On the way back to the hotel, we detoured to find the Baseball Hall of Fame. It backs onto an abandoned farm at the edge of town, with an old windmill marking the site of the original well.

Cooperstown it's not. The tourist guide identifies the tiny building only as the oldest church in town, but giant baseball bats on the front lawn indicate its current use. The door was locked, with a note posted saying that it would be open in the afternoon.

To complete the grand tour, we located the Legion Hall where the luncheon was scheduled and the Community Centre for dinner. We drove back across the river valley that separates Battleford from North Battleford, which turned out to have a main street filled with vacant stores, pawn shops, and other indicators of hard times. The life of the town had moved to the mall on the highway across from our hotel.

The phone rang the moment we got back into the room. My mother, worried.

"It's a five-minute drive," I said. "We'll meet you in the lobby in ten minutes. Did Sheila get here yet?"

"They just walked in."

"Good. We'll see you in the lobby."

When I got off the phone, Andy handed me a shot of Scotch in a plastic glass.

"I know it's early, but I figured we could use it."

We clicked glasses and downed the drinks in one gulp.

"I'm ready for anything now," he said, then reconsidered. "Except perhaps another dinner with Uncle Stan and Auntie Merle."

CHAPTER

6

The lunch reminded me of socials in the old church basement when I was young. The Legion Hall was an unassuming building on Battleford's main street with a hand-lettered welcome sign on an easel on the pavement outside the building. There was a coat rack inside the door, where we left our dripping umbrellas before presenting ourselves at the reception table. My mother was given a tag with her name written in elaborate calligraphy. Underneath, as an afterthought that rather spoiled the effect, the word "inductee" had been added in ballpoint pen.

The rest of us were left to fend for ourselves while one of the hostesses took my parents away to meet people. We hung around looking at strangers and caught up with each other's lives.

My sister, Sheila, is one of those busy women. She raises the kids, keeps the ranch books, and works at the library, while still finding time to volunteer at a sheltered workshop and sing in the church choir. I, in the meantime, barely manage one job. I don't volunteer. I don't do good works. I don't even go to church, and Andy's lucky if I make dinner more than once a week, even in the off-season.

It goes without saying that I am reduced to a simmering stew of equal parts love, inadequacy, and resentment whenever I'm in her orbit. Her kids and I have a great time together, but I feel as if she thinks I set a bad example.

Her husband, Buddy, is a cattleman, happiest working with his stock or talking with his cronies. He's a big wheel in the Saskatchewan Stockgrowers Association. He's a small, stringy kind of guy, in contrast with my sister, who carries a few extra pounds on her hips. He's more at home on saddle leather than on chintz, but he clearly worships Sheila and the girls, even if their feminine world is not one he understands.

The girls, Amy, who is eleven, and Claire, nine, were on their best behaviour, wearing pretty sundresses – made by Sheila, of course – and brightly coloured sandals. Although they were probably bored with all the adults in the room, most of whom would qualify for discounts at the movie house, they were silenced by the sense of occasion. They stuck to me like a pair of adoring puppies, and cast flirtatious glances at Andy, whom they thought terribly glamorous.

After a while, we headed for the food table, which was covered with a paper tablecloth that had baseball stuff printed on it, bats and balls and gloves, with serviettes and paper plates to match.

There was a choice of boring sandwiches cut on the diagonal – ham, tuna, or egg salad on white bread, brown bread, or a combination of the two. There was a coffee urn, a teapot, and a pitcher of something orange that tasted unlike any actual fruit. But the pickles were homemade, and there were tasty-looking goodies for after.

We filled our paper plates and Styrofoam cups and found a place to sit down at one of the long folding tables. Sheila took a plate of sandwiches to my parents, and came back smiling.

"She's having the time of her life," she said.

"That's our Mum. Born to mingle."

"Well, it's good to see her in the spotlight for a change instead of just being wife-of."

"And it's probably good for Daddy to see how husband-of feels," I laughed.

"He doesn't look like he minds," Andy said.

"Yeah, he's plenty proud," Sheila said.

A man on my left interrupted us, a good-looking guy probably in his early fifties. A middle-aged hunk, Doreen would have said. He was lean, with deep-set blue eyes, good cheekbones, and a sensuous mouth. His hair, grey at the temples, was dark and wavy. He looked a little dangerous, the kind of man I used to fall for, before I lost my taste for trouble.

"I couldn't help overhearing," he said in the flat accent of the American Mid-West. "Is your mother one of the inductees?"

"Yes, over there, in the blue-and-white stripes," I said.

"Who did she play for?"

"The Racine Belles."

"No kidding? My mom did, too."

44

"Who's she?"

"Virna Wilton. She was the shortstop."

He pointed her out, a tall, elegant-looking woman in pants and a long, loose jacket. She wore slingback sandals. Her most striking feature was her upswept salt-and-pepper hair, with one silver streak waving back off her forehead.

"For heaven's sake," Sheila said. "She was one of Mum's best friends. Helen Henry. MacLaren, she was then."

"*Wheels* MacLaren? You're kidding!"

We introduced ourselves. He was Jack Wilton.

"You're the second person today I've heard call her that," I said. "I never even knew she had a nickname. Why did they call her Wheels? Did she steal lots of bases?"

"It was just a pun," Jack said. "You know, Helen Wheels. Hell on wheels. They used to call her Hellion, too."

"You know a lot about it," Sheila said.

"I grew up with the league. Mom was in it until the end. She moved to Fort Wayne after the Belles folded, and played with the Daisies until 1954. I was nine at the time."

"Our mother lasted five years," Sheila said. "She quit after the 1947 season to get married."

"A lot of women did that," he said.

"What about your father?" Andy asked him. "Didn't he mind his wife playing ball?"

"I didn't have a father. I mean, obviously I did, but I never knew him. He died overseas in the war. I mainly had a lot of honorary aunts."

"Did you travel around with the team?"

"Sometimes. Or I'd stay home with the landlady. It was a different way to grow up, but it suited us."

"Did you get to be a bat boy?" asked my tomboy niece Claire, who is campaigning to move to Toronto to live with us and work as the Titans' first bat girl.

"Sure. I had to earn my keep," Jack said, giving her a killer smile.

"Well, if it was girls' baseball, why didn't they have bat *girls*?" Claire asked.

"Well, they did. But since I was a boy, I had to be a bat boy, didn't I?"

"There's no such thing as a bat girl in real baseball," said Amy, whose ambition is to become a veterinarian. Specializing in horses, she says. "It's a dumb idea."

Seeing that the two were about to get into an is-not-is-too free-for-all, I suggested a dessert run. When we came back with plates full of cookies, nanaimo bars, and date squares, Andy and Jack were talking hate mail with Sheila.

"Jack's mother got letters, too," Andy said.

"Why didn't you tell us about this before?" Sheila demanded. "This is awful. We have to tell someone about this."

"I told my mother that we should go to the police," Jack said, "but she thinks it's just a joke."

"It probably is," I said. "But we should find out if anyone else got one."

"Let's go ask," Sheila said, getting up from the table. I followed her across the room to where my parents were sitting with several other players. Jack went to his mother, who was with a different group.

"I was just telling your mother about the letter I got," Edna Summers said. "I was quite frightened."

"Why, of course you would be," one of the other women said, a tall woman with gold-rimmed glasses.

Her name tag identified her as Willetta Heising, who had played for the Rockford Peaches.

"Did you get one, too?" I asked.

"No. The only ones I've heard about are the Belles."

Jack Wilton joined us at the table.

"My mother said she had heard that Shirley Goodman, the pitcher, got a letter, too," he said.

"I don't think she's here yet," Edna said. "At least I haven't seen her."

"My mother spoke to her on the phone last week," Jack said, then put out his hand. "I'm Jack Wilton, by the way."

"Edna Summers. I was Edna Adams."

"I'm very pleased to meet you. And you must be Helen Henry. I've heard a lot about you. Both from your charming daughters and my own mother."

"Well. Nice to meet you," my mother said, a little rudely, I thought, then turned to my father. "I think we should be getting back to the hotel, don't you, Douglas?"

She stood up.

"Excuse me, please," she said. "I'll just see to the little girls."

She was turning to walk away when the room was pierced by a loud whistle. Once he had got our attention, a jokey gentleman in a plaid shirt introduced himself as a vice-president of the Hall of Fame board and announced that the museum was open and that we were all welcome to visit.

"Do you want to go?" I asked my mother.

"Oh, you mustn't," Edna explained. "We Belles are all waiting until tomorrow, after the induction."

"Once it's official, you mean," I said. "That makes sense. What do you want to do instead?"

47

"I'll just go back to the hotel," she said. "I think your father wants to rest his hip a bit, and we've got a big night ahead of us."

"Did someone mention going to the police?" Edna asked.

"I think someone should," I agreed and we moved towards the door.

"I'd be happy to go," Jack said. "What about you, Andy? It might be good to have a policeman along, too."

"That's a good idea," my sister said. "They'll listen to you."

Andy looked trapped.

"You don't have to," I said.

"That's fine."

"Do you want me to come?"

"No, I don't want to make a big production of this. Do you have the letter with you?"

I dug it out of my bag and gave it to him.

"You're sure you don't mind?"

"It's not like I've got anything better to do."

CHAPTER

7

Andy took Jack with him in our purple rental car, which the nieces had by now dubbed the Grapemobile, and followed the tourist map to the Battlefords Royal Canadian Mounted Police detachment across the river in North Battleford. It was an unadorned two-storey brick building a couple of blocks off the main street into town.

It was apparently a slow crime day. Inspector Walter Digby, the top cop, invited the two into his office, standard Mountie issue, including the portrait of Her Majesty gazing down upon them from the wall behind the desk.

Andy and Jack had decided on the way over that Andy would do the talking, cop to cop. He and Inspector Digby began by exploring the possibility of mutual law enforcement friends, and came up with several to break the ice. Andy had been on a forensics course ten years before with Digby's former partner, and Digby had gone to

RCMP training college in Regina with a Mountie Andy had worked with on a series of drug-related murders in overlapping jurisdictions in Ontario.

That out of the way, like a secret handshake in a fraternal order, Digby dropped his social tone and inquired about the reason for the visit. Andy told him about the letters.

"Since they were postmarked here in the Battlefords, I thought you might have some usual suspects in your files."

"Do you have letters with you?" Digby asked.

"Just the one Mrs. Henry got yesterday," Andy said, putting it on the desk. "She threw out the previous one, but her description is consistent with it being the same writer."

"It looks like the one my mother got, too," Jack said.

Digby studied the letter. He appeared to be around Andy's age, in the mid-forties, but might as well have come from a different generation altogether. What hair he had was trimmed short and combed neatly, and he had one of those trim toothbrush moustaches that put one in mind of World War Two officers. He was in full uniform, and everything about him was tidy, from the polish on his shoes to the rigidly aligned stacks of paper on his desk. Disorder did not appear to be a permissible option in his life.

He folded the letter, picked up the phone, and punched in three numbers.

"Got a minute? In my office," he said, then hung up.

A moment later, there was a knock on the door, immediately followed by the entrance of a compact, clean-shaven man, probably in his mid-thirties, with a dark brown buzz cut and friendly brown eyes. He was also in uniform, but without a jacket or tie. After introducing Staff Sergeant Michael Morris, Digby gave him the letter and explained the circumstances under which it arrived.

"So who got these letters?" Morris asked. "All the women?"

"Apparently not," Andy said. "It seems to have been sent to women who played together on one particular team, the Racine Belles."

The phone on Digby's desk buzzed. He picked it up, listened for a moment, then punched the hold button.

"I'll let you take it from here, Mickey," he said, then held out his hand to each of the visitors in turn. "Thank you for bringing this to our attention."

"That's it?" Jack interjected. "Isn't there something we should be doing to protect these women?"

"There will be representatives of the Force in attendance this evening, both in a ceremonial and a personal capacity," Digby said. "Including my wife and myself. The induction dinner is one of the high points of our year in the Battlefords. I'll keep my eyes open, as will the other officers there."

Morris led the other two to the door.

"By the way, Mickey," Digby said, "please extend Inspector Munro every professional courtesy. He is with the Metropolitan Toronto Police Department."

Andy couldn't tell if he was making fun of him or not, but decided to let it pass. From his years with me, he knew that mocking big-city airs ranks right up there with hockey, CFL football, and curling as favourite provincial pastimes.

Morris seemed friendly enough, though. He took them through the story again, then led the two into another office.

"This is Sergeant Deutsch," he said, of an altogether hipper-looking cop sitting with his cowboy boots up on his cluttered desk. He was throwing darts at a picture of the actor Paul Gross, dressed in the red serge he wears as the straight-arrow Mountie on "Due South".

Despite his rather disreputable appearance, Deutsch turned out to be the head of the plainclothes General Investigation Section, which handled all major crimes in the area.

"Threats don't normally fall under Donny's jurisdiction," Morris explained, "but he's blessed with a mind that's halfway between an encyclopedia and a fully loaded computer."

He handed the letter to Deutsch, who still hadn't taken his feet off the desk.

"What do you make of this?"

The Sergeant glanced at it and shrugged.

"Typical crank," he said. "Who got it?"

Jack explained about his mother, the Hall of Fame, and the other women who had received the same kind of thing.

"Thought you might have a possible perp in your mental files," Morris said.

"Not offhand. You say they were sent from here?"

"Look at the postmark."

He did.

"Could be some nutbar out at the mental hospital," he said, handing the letter to Morris. "I wouldn't worry about it."

"Don's right," Morris said. "Ninety-nine times out of a hundred, these kinds of letters are nothing to worry about. But, like the Inspector said, we'll keep our eyes open tonight. My wife and I are going, too. My uncle from Kindersley was inducted in there five years ago, and we always go to the dinner. It's a nice event, and Dave Shury, who organizes the deal, is a popular man in town. So, if there's any trouble at all, we'll be on the scene."

"So the women shouldn't be worried, then?" Jack asked.

"I don't think so, but you were right to let us know," Morris said.

"Thanks for your time," Andy said. "We can find our way out."

"No trouble. I'll see you tonight then."

Going back through the central office area, Andy was struck by the laid-back atmosphere of the small-town cop-shop. There was none of the tension and energy he was used to in Toronto. It felt downright good-natured. A week here, he thought, would drive him nuts.

Outside, the rain had stopped, and the puddles were steaming in the afternoon sunshine.

"They didn't seem too concerned," Jack said.

"No. I didn't think they would be."

"We've done our duty, though, and it will reassure the women."

"Duty done, it's probably time for a beer," Andy said.

"Lead the way. I've been thirsty for a Canadian brew since I got here."

CHAPTER

8

While Andy and Jack Wilton were with the RCMP, I put in some family time by the hotel pool with my mother and sister. My father had gone to their room to lie down. The girls were having a grand time on the slides. Amy, who is at the awkward age between childhood and adolescence, had opted for the former for the afternoon, and her giggles and shrieks outdid even Claire's.

"It's good to see them," I said to Sheila. "They're growing up too fast."

"I know. Sometimes I wish I could just freeze them at the age they are now. The next phase is going to be hell. Amy's going to be a teenager, and Claire's going to feel left behind."

"It happened with us," I agreed.

"But it worked out in the end," my mother said. "And the girls will be fine, too."

"Things are different now, Mum," Sheila said. "We

grew up in innocent times. The temptations are more dangerous now. The stakes are higher."

"You'll survive it, Sheila dear," our mother said. "After all, I did."

My sister and I exchanged a look, and laughed.

"But you didn't know half of what we were up to," I said. "And what you did know about, you disapproved of."

"I don't think that's fair," she said.

"Well, you didn't disapprove of Sheila, that's true," I jibed. "She was Miss Perfect."

"I had to be, with you misbehaving all over the place," she said. "It was such a burden."

"Burden? What about my burden?" I said. "I had to follow in your footsteps all through school. All the teachers thought I was going to be just like you, and I disappointed every one of them."

"That's true," Sheila said, smugly. We both laughed.

"Stop it, the two of you," our mother said. "I am proud of both of you, in different ways. Even if you did try me sorely from time to time."

Claire's arrival put an end to our ritual spat. She was shivering and blue-lipped. Sheila wrapped a towel around her.

"It's the funnest, Mum," she said. "You should try it. The slide. You too, Kate."

"I'll pass," I said. I hadn't changed into my bathing suit. I prefer to do my swimming in fresh lakes, out of doors.

"Besides, I think you've had enough," Sheila said. "I want you both to have a rest. You've got a late night coming up, and I don't want you to be cranky."

"Get serious," Claire said. "I'm not taking any nap."

"I didn't say you had to nap. I just want you to have some quiet time," Sheila said.

"Just ten more slides, please?" Claire bargained.

"Five."

"Seven and a half?" Claire countered.

"If you can do half a slide, I want to be there to see it," Sheila laughed. "Go ahead, but tell Amy it's almost time to pack it in."

As Claire ran off, calling to her sister, Edna Summers rolled up with her walker.

"Is this a private family session, or can I join you?"

"Of course," my mother said. "Sheila, get Edna a chair."

Ever obedient, Sheila was up before she finished asking.

"I got bored in my room, so I thought I'd see what trouble I could find down here," Edna said. "I was watching the ball game, but the Titans were already up six runs in the second inning."

I looked at my watch. It was only three, but with the time difference, the four o'clock game was already an hour old.

"Do you think I could get a cup of tea?" Edna asked.

I beat Sheila to it this time.

"I'll go see what I can do," I said, jumping up. On my way into the restaurant, I ran into Andy and Jack.

"Hey, Kate," Jack said. "Want to join us for a beer?"

"I'd love to, but tea is the order of the day by the pool. What did the Mounties have to say?"

"They said not to worry about it," Andy said. "For what it's worth."

"Good. See what you can do to reassure Mum and the others. I'll get the beers."

56

I found a waitress and placed our orders, then went back to the table. My mother and Edna had been joined by another couple. The wife was large and sturdy-looking, with her hair cut into a short, no-nonsense style. Her husband was tall and lanky, with the look, and tan, of a farmer, the skin on his forehead paler than the rest of his weathered face.

"Kate, this is Margaret Deneka and her husband, Peter," my mother said. "We used to call her Meg the Peg when she played third base for the Belles."

"Because of her great arm," Edna explained.

Mrs. Deneka grinned and made a quick, graceful throwing movement with her right arm. Her husband smiled fondly at her, but his look was also faintly worried.

"Please sit down and join us," my mother said.

"Shall we, Peter?"

"I think you should rest," he said. "You have a big night tonight. You know, the banquet."

"He takes good care of me," she said. "My mind isn't what it used to be, you know, sometimes I forget things. It's so nice to see all the girls, I feel like I'm twenty-five again. But I'll just follow orders."

"Before you go, Mrs. Deneka," Jack said, "I wanted to ask you if you got any strange letters lately. About this induction."

A frown crossed her face.

"I don't think so," she said, then peered up at her husband. "Dear? Did I get any letters?"

"No, nothing like that," he said, then threw Jack a quick glance and a small nod. "We'd better be going now. Have that little nap."

"All right," she said. "We'll be toddling along now. We'll have plenty of chances to chat later. Lovely to see you, Edna. And you too, Helen. Is Carl with you?"

"Carl? Oh, you mean my husband, Douglas? Yes, he's just resting now."

"Oh, yes, Douglas. What was I thinking of?"

She tapped her forehead. "Just this pesky brain of mine," she said. "Time to give it a rest."

She took her husband's arm and gave us a little finger flutter of a wave.

"See you later. Toodle-oo."

We waited until she left.

"She got a letter, all right," Jack said. "The old dear just forgot it."

"More likely her husband kept it from her," I said. "I'll ask him about it later."

"It's all very well for you young people," my mother said, with surprising anger. "Making fun of someone because she's old. She used to be smarter than any of you. When you're old, I hope you remember this moment and feel badly."

She got up and left the table. Sheila and I looked at each other in astonishment.

"I don't know what got into her," I said to Jack. "This isn't like her."

"She's right, you know," Edna said. "You could have put it a bit more diplomatically."

"But still," I said. "She's not usually so, well, blunt."

"Blunt? She was downright rude," Sheila said.

"She's probably more nervous about the letters than she's saying," Andy said.

"And about the big night in the spotlight," I added.

"We're all a little nervous," Edna agreed.

We were interrupted by a great shriek from the girls in the pool. We looked over in time to see Virna Wilton, in a bright pink suit and a flowered bathing cap, spiralling down the biggest slide to land with a great splash.

"And then, there's my mother," Jack said, shaking his head.

CHAPTER

9

The forty-ounce poodle was Andy's undoing. The grand prize in the raffle for the Baseball Hall of Fame, it sat on a table, its little pink crochet head tilted to one side, its little pink crochet front paws raised. The crochet body cunningly concealed a bottle of rye, and Andy lost control the moment he set eyes upon it. He stood in the middle of the Battleford Community Recreation Centre fighting off the giggles, with tears of laughter filling his eyes. I socked him on the arm.

"Stop it," I whispered, trying not to lose control myself. "Someone will notice."

"I have to get a ticket. I've got to win the poodle."

"Not until you stop laughing. That nice woman selling them probably made it herself. She'll think you're laughing at her."

He wiped his eyes with the back of his hand.

"I'm not laughing at her," he said, back under control. "I'm laughing at the concept."

"No you're not. You're laughing at Saskatchewan, and as far as I'm concerned, that means you're laughing at me. And I don't like being laughed at, Mister."

He put his hand on my shoulder and gave me his most sincere look, laughter still in his eyes.

"I'm not laughing at you or the province that made you the wonderful woman you are today. I promise."

"Apology accepted, even if it wasn't, technically, offered."

"Good," he said, taking my hand to shake it. "We're friends again. Now can we buy a ticket? I've got to have that poodle."

The tickets themselves nearly set him off one more time. They were playing cards. When we had each selected one, the woman selling them tore them in half and gave one piece to us and put the other into a goldfish bowl. Andy got the nine of clubs from the Grey Cup commemorative deck; I got the joker from the deck with the bunnies. He stuck them in his pocket and we went to find the bar.

Amy and Claire found us first, Claire skittering through the crowd like a running back looking for daylight, Amy following at a more sedate, grown-up, pace.

"We got tickets, and Mum said we could have pop!" Claire said. "Can you come with us to get it?"

"Walk this way," I said, bending my knees and pointing my feet in opposite directions. Claire, giggling, waddled after me. Amy and Andy looked at each other and rolled their eyes.

There was a crowd at the bar, a service counter between the tiny galley kitchen and the main hall.

"I've got the elbows for this job," Andy said. "What do you want?"

Cokes for the girls. Vodka and tonic for me. He was back in a few minutes with four glasses, two of them empty.

"Pop's free, so I got us doubles. Mix is over on a table in the corner, he said."

As it turned out, there was no tonic, just Coke and Sprite in two-litre bottles, a bucket of ice, a pitcher of water, and another with orange stuff I recognized from lunch.

I put some ice in my plastic glass, then raised it to Andy.

"I'll pretend it's a martini," I said. "Very dry. What have you got?"

"Rye," he said, reaching for the Sprite. "What else."

Jack Wilton came up behind us, with Edna Summers holding his arm with one hand and a sturdy, four-footed cane with the other. Edna was a round cloud of pink ruffles, and Jack was handsome and sort of country-club American in a blue blazer and chinos.

"Hello, all," Edna said. "Isn't this exciting?"

"Hi, Mrs. Summers," Claire said. "You look pretty."

"Thank you, dear, so do you. You, too, Amy."

"What about me?" Andy joked.

"You look lovely, too."

"Where is your mother?" I asked Jack. "I hope the water slide didn't do her in."

"Not a chance," he smiled. "I have to go back and pick

her up. She wasn't quite ready, and Edna didn't want to wait."

"I need a little more time with this darned stick," she said. "But I was for sure not going to roll into the Hall of Fame on a walker. Besides, Virna's never been on time for anything in her life. We always used to call her 'the late Virna Wilton.' Besides, she just wants to make a big entrance."

"Edna, you promised not to give anything away," Jack said.

The former catcher smiled and winked at Claire, then locked her lips with an imaginary key.

"Now, Jack, maybe you could turn this ticket they gave me at the door into a rye and Seven."

"Are you all right for a minute on your own?"

"Don't be silly," she said. "I'm fine. It's just the knees. If I need to sit down, Kate will get me to a chair."

"We'll be over by the display area," I said to Jack, pointing across the room where my parents and some of the other players were gathered.

"What table are you at?" Edna asked, as we made our way.

"Table thirteen," Amy said. "That's the Belles table, so we're all there."

"Not me or your Gram," Edna said. "Or Jack's mum either. We're sitting up there at the head table. That's because tonight we're the most important people in the room. What do you think about that?"

"Cool," Claire said.

"Cool as a cucumber," Edna agreed. Claire giggled. Amy rolled her eyes again.

The head table was raised along the far end of the long room. Arranged below it were two ranks of long tables, each made up with white linen and flower centre-pieces with blue candles in them to match the crêpe-paper streamers draped from the girders in the ceiling and the balloons taped to the walls. It looked as if it had been decorated by the prom committee at a school for the imaginationally challenged. Some tables were already full of eager-looking people. Past their supper-time, no doubt.

"I wonder which one is unlucky thirteen?" Andy wondered.

"Over there," Claire pointed. "Mum and me saved seats for everyone."

"You should have said 'Mum and I' saved seats," Amy said. Claire stuck out her tongue.

"She's right," I said. "But whoever did it, it was thoughtful. Thank you."

In the display area, there were large photographs of each of the women being inducted as well as scrapbooks and other memorabilia that had been donated to the Hall of Fame.

"Isn't that your bat, Edna?" my mother asked, as we joined them. "It's got your number on the handle."

"That's the one that beat the Peaches," she said. "That's the one that hit the home run."

"And you're giving it to the museum?"

"It might as well be here as in the garbage after I die."

"Please, let's not be morbid," my mother fussed. "It's a night for celebration."

"Nothing morbid about thinking about death," Edna said cheerfully. "It's going to come to all of us sooner or later. In our cases, Helen, sooner. Can't pretend otherwise."

Jack came up and handed her a glass.

"I'm going to get Mom," he said. "Can you see that Edna gets to where she has to go, Kate?"

"Of course," I said. "We'll see you in a few minutes."

"Where do you have to be, Edna?" Andy asked.

"Oh, there's some kind of official picture being taken at six o'clock. I don't know where."

"I do," my mother said, looking at her watch. "We've got fifteen minutes yet."

Another couple joined us then. The woman was wearing a long dress in bold vertical black-and-red stripes, which served to emphasize, rather than hide, the cruel curve of her spine from osteoporosis. But her infirmity didn't stop her from making an effort. Her bleached blonde hair was done in an elaborate helmet with kiss curls at the temples, and she was in full glamour makeup of an earlier era. Her gloomy-looking husband, who was even shorter than she, wore a black blazer with gold buttons and a bowtie that matched the red of her dress. I recognized them as a couple I'd seen checking in in the lobby earlier, dressed in matching Hawaiian shirts.

"Shirley and Bert Goodman," my mother said in introduction, "This is my husband, Reverend Douglas Henry, and our daughter, Kate, and her . . friend, Inspector Andy Munro."

She paused only for a small, disapproving, beat, but I heard it. I smiled and shook hands with the Goodmans.

"Shirley was our star pitcher," my mother said. "She led the league in wins in 1945."

"Now, tell me right away," Shirley said, "tell me if you are the one who writes the baseball for the *Toronto Planet*."

I admitted it.

"I knew it, didn't I, Bert? Didn't I always say that she must be Helen's daughter? Didn't I always say that? That she must be Helen Henry's daughter because she surely does know her ball. I must have said that a hundred times."

"At least, dear," her husband said. He was wearing a hearing aid in his right ear. I wondered how often he turned it off.

"Well, I'm just thrilled to meet you," Shirley went on. "I read your write-ups every day. We live in Etobicoke, you see, so we're *Planet* readers. Aren't we, Bert?"

He didn't bother to agree, just took another mournful drink.

"How long have you lived in Ontario?" I asked.

"Most of our married life, haven't we, Bert? We moved just after our wedding in 1950, and we have enjoyed our bliss there ever since. This is our first trip back in years."

"How nice," I said, for want of anything more intelligent.

"I was just saying to your mother how wonderful it is to get the gals together like this again. I keep up through the newsletter, but it's not the same. And I say it's about time this Hall of Fame recognized us. We're getting our due too late. What about poor Wilma Elshaw? She died five months ago."

"I met her brother this afternoon," Mum said. "He's here to represent her. That's him over there, in the blue suit."

She pointed to a tall, slightly stooped man with glasses, standing with a group of men by the bar. He was the only one not laughing. He looked fit, considering his age.

"Didn't she come from around here somewhere?" Shirley said. "I think I remember that she did."

"Yes, right here in Battleford," my mother said, "but she made her home in Indiana."

"Well, of course, she did. I knew that. And who else is here? We just got in this afternoon. Is dear Virna here?"

"Her son's just gone to get her," I said.

"She'd best hurry, they're going to want us for the group photograph soon," my mother said.

We suddenly became aware of a commotion across the room, by the door. Edna looked up and laughed.

"Never fear, Virna's here. And how!"

We all turned to see Virna Wilton make her entrance, dressed in a goldenrod-yellow Racine Belles uniform, with her head held high and a grin all over her face. Jack at her side, she waved both arms over her head to acknowledge the applause that erupted at the sight of her. The Goodmans went towards her, but the rest of us stayed back to watch.

"Darn her, anyway, she can still fit into it," Edna muttered.

"That's what they wore?" Amy asked, momentarily startled out of her world-weary pose. "Skirts to play baseball?"

"We wore skirts for everything back then," my mother said. "Ladies didn't wear pants."

"And the league wanted to make sure everyone knew we were ladies," Edna laughed. "We wanted to play in pants, but they stuck us with those stupid uniforms. You couldn't even slide in them without losing half the skin on your legs. I've still got scars. Mind you, Virna always did wear hers a little shorter than regulations, as you can see. But, darn her, she's still got the legs for it, at her age."

"The ballplayers always say the legs are the first to go," I mused. "But in women, they're what last the longest."

"At least she's not wearing her spikes," Edna said.

"I don't think the floors would take it," I said, noting that she had compromised with black leather high-top Reeboks that went well with the knee-length socks and didn't look too incongruously modern.

"I don't know where she gets her nerve," my mother said. "I could never do such a thing."

"She always had nerve, Helen," Edna answered. "Virna Wilton never lacked for nerve."

"We'd better be getting to the other room for pictures, Edna," my mother said, looking at her watch. "We'll see you all later."

"Good luck, dear," my father said. "You look lovely tonight."

And she did, in a pretty flowered suit of some soft synthetic material she'd bought in Regina for the occasion. She excused her extravagance by reminding herself she could wear it to a wedding they were attending in September.

"Knock 'em dead, Mum," I said. "You too, Edna."

But they were already gone, Edna holding on to my mother's arm. Two extraordinary women on their way to the moment of their lives.

CHAPTER

10

Like most couples, Andy and I can read each other's minds, and seen through his urban eyes, the whole scene – the pathetic decorations; the forty-ounce poodle; the old team photos glued to bristol board; the hairdos, the clothes; the hearty back-slapping laughter of the men at the bar; the assembly of eccentric women in corsages with their nicknames and their jokes that were corny the first time around, fifty years before – was hokey beyond anything he'd ever seen in Toronto, even in hard-core suburbia. It was un-cool, un-hip, un-chic. It was un-Toronto. There wasn't a leaf of radicchio in sight.

But I feared that he could never see the scene as I saw it: a community ritual, a clan gathering of decent people, genuinely warm and friendly, so downright nice, so like the folks who crowd my memories of childhood. These are my people, and I resented Andy for making me embarrassed to be one of them. When the pianist played

69

"When the Saints Go Marching In" and the head table guests entered behind an RCMP constable in ceremonial red serge and everybody at all the tables stood up and clapped in rhythm, I could barely see Mum through the tears of pride.

We stayed on our feet to sing 'O Canada' (in English only), and to receive the benediction from the local Catholic priest. We toasted Her Majesty the Queen. We sat down.

The master of ceremonies for the evening was a skinny little guy with a three-ball voice and a fuzzy moustache, who turned out to be the program director at a local private radio station and clearly something of a Battleford celebrity. He certainly had a face for radio. After welcoming us, he explained that dinner would be served buffet-style, in order of table number, starting with Table One. There were loud groans and laughter from everybody on our side of the room.

Then the emcee introduced the head table, and asked for a moment of silence in honour of deceased Hall of Fame members. Then he mentioned the notable guests: a former leader of the provincial Conservative Party, five previous inductees, the local federal member of parliament (a New Democrat, I was pleased to note), two aldermen, the mayor of North Battleford, and, of course, Inspector Digby. The biggest hand was for Dave Shury, chairman of the Hall of Fame, a good-looking older man who acknowledged the applause from a wheelchair.

"That Dave's quite a guy," said the man on my right, round as a doughnut and bald as an egg. "I guess you know him."

I admitted that I hadn't had the pleasure.

"Oh, well, you have to meet him. Without him, there wouldn't be a Hall of Fame. There wouldn't even be a Saskatchewan Baseball Association. He's our guiding genius, afflicted as he is. He can do more from that chair than any two able-bodied men."

"It's certainly impressive," I agreed. "I'm Kate Henry, by the way. My mother was a Belle. Is your wife one of the players?"

"Oh, no. Never had one of them. I came along with my pal Garth Elshaw. He's up there on the platform representing his late sister Wilma, may she rest in peace. Morley Timms is the name."

I shook his hand and introduced those in our group within earshot, including my father, Claire, Andy, and Jack Wilton, who was across the table from Timms.

"Well, then I guess you knew Wilma, too," Timms said.

"Of course," Jack said. "She was my mother's best friend. And she was like a second mother to me."

He turned to me.

"My mother and Aunt Wilma had a business together in Fort Wayne after their playing days were over. The All-American All-Star Flower Shoppe. Two *p*s and an *e*. They thought it was classier that way. Wilma did the arrangements and Mom ran the business. And we all lived in the apartment above the store."

"My condolences to you on your loss," Timms said.

"Thank you," Jack said, then explained to me. "Aunt Wilma died of cancer in March. Just after we heard about the Hall of Fame. So at least she knew."

He had bought a bottle of wine, and he poured some for me, then motioned it towards the older man's empty glass.

"No thanks," he said. "Don't indulge. Haven't touched the stuff in more than forty years."

He turned to me and tapped his temple.

"Keep the head clear, and anything's possible," he said. "That's my motto."

"And an admirable one it is," my father said. "By the way, have you met Bert Goodman, on the other side of you?"

The two shook hands, and Goodman muttered a greeting. Peter Deneka was across the table, and I introduced him to my father.

"It's nice to see so many of you here," Deneka said.

"We've taken over the table, I'm afraid," my father said.

"Well, that's a good thing," Deneka said. "It's good you're so proud of her. Our kids couldn't be here. Too far to come. Our son's in Ontario, working for the Hydro there, and the daughter sells real estate in British Columbia."

"That's the way it is these days," my father said. "All the young people move away."

"That's the truth, but who can blame them? There's nothing for them here. My son didn't want to be a farmer," Deneka said. "I don't know why not. You freeze in the winter, broil in the summer, and work seven days a week just to pay the interest on your bank loan. That's if the gophers and grasshoppers don't get your crop."

He laughed heartily. Farmer humour.

"Where do you farm?" Timms asked.

"I don't any more," he said. "My wife hasn't been well, and what with no one to help me run it, I sold and moved into town. To Esterhazy, for the hospital and all."

"We're from over that way, too," my father said. "We're in Indian Head."

"Well, you got yourself some baseball history over there. Did you ever play?"

My father laughed.

"No, that was my wife's department. I never had the athletic talent."

"I remember those tournaments they had there, back in the fifties. They'd draw ten thousand people. That's when they had those Negro players Jimmy Robison brought up from the south. Oh, he was a smart one, all right. The Indian Head Rockets. Didn't they just win everything for a while there?"

"That was before my time in Indian Head," Daddy said. "I've heard about it, of course, but I never saw them play."

"That's too bad. Those were good times. I saw some pictures of those teams over at the Hall of Fame this afternoon. Surely brought back memories."

"We haven't gone yet," I said. "We're going over tomorrow. I think there's a plan for all the Belles to go together."

"Yes, I know about that. At eleven," Deneka said. "We'll be there. And, look, it's finally our turn at the trough."

The people from the table behind us were returning with full plates. We stood up. Morley Timms helped me with my chair.

"Ladies first," he said.

CHAPTER

II

The keynote speech was an apparent inning-by-inning history of the All-American Girls Professional Baseball League, delivered by a sports historian from Winnipeg. Her research was commendable, but her delivery was dismal. When she finally wound down, the applause was delivered more out of gratitude than appreciation.

Her audience, at least the part of it in my immediate vicinity, was suffering from the torpor that comes after a big meal. We had been fed chicken in a vaguely oriental sauce, with mushroom rice, corn niblets, and several salads, along with dinner rolls. Dessert was strawberry shortcake, with whipped cream from a can. By the time the speech was over, our coffee cups were empty, the dessert plates were sticky, and I was dying for a smoke and a pee, not necessarily in that order. I was about to sneak out when the master of ceremonies went to the podium.

"Now for the moment we've all been waiting for," he said. "In a just a few minutes, the Saskatchewan Baseball Hall of Fame will have received twenty new members, twenty new *female* members, into its honoured ranks."

"It's about time, too," a woman shouted from the back of the room, to the obvious amusement of the head table.

I apologized to my bladder, and promised not to feed it any more coffee if it would just behave itself for another half-hour.

"Our first honouree hails from the town of Watrous. For six years, she backed up the plate for the Racine Belles . . ."

As he introduced her, a grinning Edna Summers stood up and was escorted slowly from the table by a well-set-up young usher in a pale blue tuxedo. He brought her to centre stage in front of the head table, where the video camera was set up.

"Three times an all-star, she will always be remembered for the home run she hit off Gull Lake's own Willetta Heising to win the 1946 championship over the Rockford Peaches."

Great laughter, as, on the dais, the guilty party put her head down on her folded arms and pretended to cry.

"Because Edna Summers was Edna Adams during most of her career, she alphabetically qualifies to become the first woman to be inducted into the Saskatchewan Baseball Hall of Fame. I present Edna Adams Summers."

"Way to go Edna," came the shout from the woman heckler at the back, followed by applause.

"Please, ladies and gentlemen, hold your applause until all the inductees have been announced," the radio guy said. "Unless you want to be here all night."

Andy leaned over to me.

"You mean we haven't already been?"

The emcee waited for Edna to be photographed receiving her plaque, and then went on to the next player, a catcher for the Peaches, who was, in turn, escorted to the place of honour.

With applause obediently withheld, the induction moved quickly along, each woman, or the one accepting on her behalf, receiving her plaque and posing for a commemorative two-shot. Some were shy and hesitant, others bold and brassy. When it was my mother's turn, she stood shyly, but with her head held high. Claire couldn't restrain herself, and shouted out, "Yay, Gram!" Sheila shushed her. I winked. Virna Wilton was the last, and after she received her plaque, she went to the podium.

"I have been asked to respond on behalf of all the girls here tonight," she said. "I am honoured to have been chosen. Of course it's probably because I'm the last one up."

Chuckles all around. Virna was the most famous of them all, the one who made the cover of *Life* magazine the year the league was founded.

"It's been quite a day," she continued. "Meeting with my team-mates and our former foes, talking about the good old days, has been a wonderful experience. But above all, to be recognized by the Saskatchewan Baseball Hall of Fame committee as a part of the baseball history of our home province is especially sweet.

"As most of you know, I don't live here any more. With my friend and colleague Wilma Elshaw, I stayed on in Fort Wayne after the league folded and we made a business and a home for ourselves. I'm sorry she couldn't be with us tonight."

Her voice faltered, just for a moment. I looked at Jack, who was staring intently at her, tense in his chair, willing her to make it through. She smiled at him, then continued.

"Her brother, Garth, and I were speaking earlier about what kind of message she would have wanted me to deliver on her behalf. Because she exemplified the spirit of our league. She was tenacious, determined, and full of life and the sense of fun that surrounded everything she did. I think she would have wanted to say that the All-American Girls Professional Baseball League gave meaning to her life, as it did to the lives of all of us here. That it wasn't easy way back then to pull up roots and chase a dream, but it was worth it. Some called us crazy, many said it wasn't a womanly thing to do. But we did it anyway, and in doing it, changed our lives forever. And tonight, we thank you all for the honour you have given us, and are proud that we showed them what players from Saskatchewan are made of. Thank you very much."

The applause started at the head table and spread around the room, but she put up her hand for quiet.

When the room fell silent again, she squared her shoulders in her Belles uniform and began to sing, in a clear and true soprano voice.

"Batter up. Hear that call. The time has come for one and all. To play ball."

Behind her, the other women pushed back their chairs to stand and join her. Edna Summers made her way to the piano, sat down at the bench, and began to play the peppy tune.

"For we're the members of the All-American League.
We come from cities near and far.
We have Canadians, Irishmen, and Swedes.
We're one for all, we're all for one,
We're All-American."

The audience began clapping in rhythm, the women at the table linked arms.

"Each Girl holds her head so proudly high,
Her motto do or die.
She's not the one to use or need an alibi.
Our chaperones are not too soft and they're not
    too tough,
We've got a president who really knows his stuff.
We're one for all, we're all for one,
We're All-American."

As bad as the song was, they sang it wonderfully. When they had sung it twice through, the women on the dais milled around, hugging and laughing. The stand-ins, like Garth Elshaw, looked embarrassed, but pleased to be part of it all.

"Look at your mother," Andy said. "She's flying high."

She was a woman I had never seen before, her Mrs.-the-Reverend dignity thrown out the window that memory had opened. All of them looked younger than they had when they first came into the room. They *were* younger, because they had all stepped through memory's window.

The formal part of the evening wasn't quite over. The emcee stepped back to the podium to thank everyone.

Then, as is apparently traditional at the induction banquet, we finished with one last song: what else, but "Take Me Out to the Ball Game." Everybody stood, clasped hands, and swayed back and forth and sang with great gusto. I know I did. So did my father, and Sheila and the girls. Damned if that corny song didn't catch even Andy up into its spell.

Once it was over, I excused myself quickly and headed for the Ladies' room. As I left it, I saw Jack Wilton, on his way out of the Men's. Spontaneously, we hugged each other. He had a nice hard body, and he held on a moment too long.

"You must be so proud of your mother," I said.

"Wasn't she something else?"

Morley Timms came out of the Men's room, and almost bumped into us.

"Upsy-daisy, excuse me! Not watching where I'm going."

"That can be dangerous," I said.

"I'm just lost in a fog," he smiled. "All those beautiful women just spin my head. Your mother's one in a million, Mr. Wilton, I've got to tell you. One in a million."

He turned to me.

"Your mother, too, of course, she's one in a million, too."

"Guess that makes them two in a million, eh, Mr. Timms?" Jack laughed.

"You got 'er, fella," he responded, then tottered off, chuckling. "Two in a million, that's a good one."

"He's quite a character," I said.

"I've never met anyone named Morley before. I've always wanted to."

"I guess it's a very Canadian name."

"We had a dog called Morley when I was a kid."

"So what happens now, do you think?" I asked.

"I suspect we're going to be around for a while yet. Could I interest you in a cocktail?"

"You've said the magic word."

He offered me his arm, with a slight bow. I took it, with a slight curtsey. The first person I saw when we sashayed back into the room was Andy. He was standing with a couple of strangers, and didn't look at all pleased, despite the pink poodle he cradled in his arms.

I steered Jack in his direction, then let go of his arm.

"I think Andy needs rescuing," I said. "He looks a bit trapped."

"Oh, those are the policemen we talked to this afternoon."

Now that I looked, I realized they both might as well have had COP stamped on their foreheads. I stepped next to Andy.

"There you are," I said, brightly. "I see you have a new friend."

Andy grinned and held the poodle out to me.

"Your prize, madame," he said.

"Mine?"

"The bunnies won."

"Congratulations," said the younger of the two men.

"Oh, yes, sorry," Andy said. "This is Staff Sergeant Mickey Morris of the Battlefords RCMP, and Inspector Walter Digby, the head of the detachment."

"It's very nice to meet you both," I said. "And I'm glad that you were right about those letters. Everything went off without a hitch."

"It did," Digby said. "It was certainly an unusual evening, but, happily, uneventful. Good evening, Mr. Wilton. Nice to see you again. Your mother is quite a woman."

"Yes, I think I've heard that sentiment before," he said.

12

"What do you think that cop meant about it being an unusual evening?" I asked Andy on the way home.

"Just what you suspect," he said. "Before you got there he was making some remarks about the suitability, or lack of it, of women in the hallowed Hall of Fame."

"I'm glad I wasn't around then."

"So am I. Believe me, so am I."

"It wasn't such a bad night, was it?" I asked. "Didn't you manage to sort of enjoy yourself?"

"Not half as much as you did. But then, I didn't have anyone at the table to flirt with."

I looked at him, waiting for some sign that he was only kidding. It didn't come.

"Andy Munro. I can't believe you're jealous."

"Who says I'm jealous? I just thought you were coming on a bit strong to Jack Wilton. In front of your family, too. I was surprised, that's all."

"I was only being friendly. I was being polite. This may be a foreign concept to you, but that's the way we do things in Saskatchewan."

"Oh, I see. Draping yourself all over some good-looking guy is just manners on the prairies. I'll try to remember that."

"I can't believe we're having this conversation," I said.

"I guess you're just a different woman when you come home to your roots," Andy continued, sarcastically. "I guess I'll just have to get to know this new, what's your euphemism? – oh, yes, *polite* – woman who homes in like a heat-seeking missile on the best-looking guy in the room and takes it upon herself to make sure that he won't forget his visit to the Saskatchewan Baseball Hall of Fame."

"All right, whatever this is really about, let's drop it," I said. "We're almost at the hotel. But, for the record, I am not *after* Jack Wilton. I think he's nice, sure. I thought you did too. But you're the only guy I want. You have been since the first day I met you. And if you don't believe that, too bad for you."

The silence lasted until we pulled into the hotel parking lot and Andy shut off the car.

"I'm sorry," he said, finally. "You're right. It's not about Jack. I'm not sure what it's about, if you want to know the truth. I guess I just feel a bit out of place here. I don't know how to fit in. And I've probably had too much to drink. So, let's just drop it for now."

"That's a deal," I said. I undid my seat belt and turned towards him. "Besides, you're cute when you're jealous."

I leaned over and kissed him. He put his arms around me awkwardly in the tiny car and turned the kiss into something more urgent, more passionate, until stray headlights lit us up.

"Maybe we better stop with the free show," I said, pulling back. "It's probably my parents."

"Oh, well, we wouldn't want to scandalize them," he said.

We got out of the car to the sound of giggles. There they all were: my parents, my sister, and the two little girls, plus Edna Summers and the Wiltons, just getting out of another car. I was glad for the darkness that hid my blushes.

"Kate and Andy, sitting in a tree," Claire chanted, in full sugar overload, "K-I-S-S-I-N-G! First comes love, then . . .

Sheila got her hand over her daughter's mouth before she got any further.

"Good party, eh, Mum?" I asked, when they caught up with us.

"It was wonderful to see all the girls again."

"See, you were worried for nothing."

"I wasn't worried. What ever gave you that idea?"

"I can't imagine," I said. "Who was it, Daddy, just the other day, who said that all the women wouldn't have anything to say to each other? It couldn't have been Mum."

"I don't know," he said. "It must have been some other person, because nobody was lacking for words tonight."

"Some of them wouldn't shut up," Sheila teased. "They had to be practically dragged out of the room."

"Stop it, all of you," my mother said. "I let my hair down for once in my life, and you aren't going to ruin it for me."

Sheila hugged her.

"No one is trying to ruin anything. We're proud of you."

"Thank you, dear. I can always count on you."

We headed for the door, and caught up with Virna, Edna, Jack, and some of the other women in the lobby.

"Come on, Helen, the girls are going to the bar, just like the old days," Virna called. "Ditch the hubby, ditch the daughters and the grandchildren. It's All-Americans only."

"Oh, I couldn't," my mother said to us.

"Why not?" my father asked.

"Sure, Mum, go ahead," I said. "It's your night."

"Well, maybe just for a few minutes."

"That's the spirit," Virna said, ushering her towards the bar.

The rest of the family got on the elevator, leaving Andy and me with Jack.

"Would you join me for a drink?" he asked.

I looked at Andy.

"You go ahead," he said. "I've had enough."

"Please don't make me drink alone," Jack said.

"I'm sorry, Jack. It's awfully late. I should go up, too."

"No, Kate, go ahead," Andy said. "It's not even mid-night, but I'm going to be asleep in about ten seconds anyway."

"Are you sure?"

He smiled at me and nodded his head.

"I'm very sure."

He kissed me and hit the elevator button.

"Just don't wake me when you come to bed."

When Jack opened the door to Shooters, the hotel lounge, the noise was formidable. It was Saturday night in small-town Saskatchewan and the joint was jumping.

Prairie Oyster was playing on the jukebox, fighting to be heard over the general racket of conversation and the electronic bells and whistles of the gambling games. I saw Garth Elshaw and Morley Timms in the crowd of locals, native and white, young and old, most in advanced stages of inebriation. It was no place for a lady, but there the whole crew of them were, in the middle of the room, having laid claim, somehow, to the best table in the house.

We made our way to the bar and grabbed a couple of empty stools as far away from the speakers as we could get. Jack got the bartender's attention, and I ordered a beer.

"Whatever's on tap and local," I shouted.

"Great Western okay?"

"Sure."

"Scotch for me," Jack yelled. "Double, lots of rocks."

"This is wild," I said, when the bartender had left. "Look at those crazy women. I can't believe my mother's with them."

"How come?"

"It's not the kind of thing she lets herself do. Fun is not her middle name."

"My mother loves a party," Jack said. "She's having the time of her life."

I looked over at the table. Virna was holding forth to some young men at the next table. I couldn't hear what she was saying over all the racket in the bar, but, judging by her gestures, she was clearly teasing them. They were spellbound and the women at the table were all laughing.

"She's probably bragging about her career," he said. "Probably challenging them to a softball game tomorrow."

"You seem fond of each other," I said.

"We're all each other has got. Especially since Aunt Wilma passed away. But even before then, we were close."

"You had an unusual upbringing, I guess."

"Yeah. It wasn't easy without a dad in the fifties."

"At least you had someone to teach you baseball," I said, "which is more than most kids of widows have."

"Oh, yes, I had that," he laughed. "Parents' sports day at school was a gas. All the other mothers were on the sidelines. Mom and Aunt Wilma were out on the field kicking butt."

I laughed.

"Other than that, it was like the conventional fifties small-town life you used to see on TV. Except ours was the Harriet and Harriet Show. No Ozzie. People were pretty tolerant, mainly. Most of them, anyway."

"What do you mean?"

"Never mind. It's not important," he said. "What about you? Where did you grow up?"

"In a little town called Indian Head, near Regina. Population 1,000, give or take. It was about as dull as you could get. I had a normal daughter-of-the-preacher kind of upbringing, and got out of there as fast as I could."

"Now you're a big-city woman."

"All the way."

"Do you ever think about coming home?"

"For about ten minutes every visit. Then something reminds me of why I left."

"It's funny. I'm the opposite. I went to the big city – Chicago – and crashed and burned. I guess I turned out to be a fish that's happiest in a smaller pond."

"Where do you live now?"

"Back home again in Indiana," he said. "Good old Fort Wayne."

"That's not Indian Head, by a long shot," I said.

"No, it's a good-sized town, over a hundred and fifty thousand."

"What do you do there?"

"I took over my mother's business."

"The flower shop?"

"What? It seems a funny job for a guy, you mean? A straight guy?"

"Whoa. I'm the last person to make gender-based judgements, remember?"

"Sorry, I guess I'm a bit defensive," he said. "Yes, I run the shop, in theory. She is supposed to be retired, but she still lives upstairs, and it's hard to keep her out of things."

"This is a problem?"

"There are certain clashes in business style, shall we say."

He signalled the bartender for another. I put my hand over my half-full pint and shook my head.

"She doesn't like change. I happen to believe that the nineties aren't the same as the fifties. We're both pretty strong-willed, so it gets tense from time to time."

"But you're obviously devoted to each other."

"Of course we are," he said. "It just doesn't look like it, sometimes. But we provide lots of amusement for the staff when we get into one of our knock-down, drag-outs."

His mother chose that moment to come and say good night.

"Look after my boy, Kate. Don't let him stay up too late."

"I'm going up soon, Mom," he said, kissing her warmly. "Sleep well. I'll see you in the morning. I'm proud of you."

I stood and held out my hand.

"I'm so glad to meet you," I said.

She ignored my hand and kissed me on the cheek.

"That goes double for me," she said. "And it's nice to see you two kids getting to know each other after all these years."

She walked away as if she had never touched a drink, head high, ignoring the other patrons, who were goggling at her Belles uniform as if they had just seen a pink elephant.

I looked at my watch.

"God, it's almost one," I said. "I'd better get going."

I took a last swallow of my beer and set it down on the bar. Jack knocked back the rest of his drink and signalled to the bartender for the bill. He insisted upon signing it to his room, then put his hand on my waist to guide me out of the bar.

"I've got a bottle in my room, if you'd like a nightcap," he said, while we waited for the elevator.

"I don't think that would be a good idea," I said.

The elevator arrived. I pushed the button for the third floor. He leaned across me to punch four.

"It's up to you," he said.

The elevator stopped at my floor with a shudder. The door opened. Jack reached out and held it back with his hand.

"Well, good night," I said. "It was nice talking to you."

He touched my cheek with his free hand and kissed me gently on the mouth, lingering for a moment before letting me go.

"It was very nice," he said then, and smiled his killer smile while the elevator doors shut. It took me a moment to decide whether I was offended by his pass. I decided, somewhat to my chagrin, that I wasn't. While I stood there regaining my composure, a door down the hall opened a crack, as if someone was peeking out. Embarrassed, I hoped that my indiscretion hadn't been observed.

I let myself into our room as quietly as I could. Andy was on the far side of the bed, asleep with his back to me. I undressed in the bathroom and crept in beside him. After a few moments, he rolled over, asleep, and curled himself around me, pinning me in his arms.

CHAPTER

13

The Hall of Fame Museum was still locked when we arrived the next morning just after eleven. Andy and I in the purple rental and my parents in the Chrysler had travelled from the hotel in convoy with the Goodmans, the Denekas and Edna Summers in Peter's mini-van. There had been no answer in either Virna or Jack Wilton's rooms, so we expected to find them waiting, but there was nobody to greet us but a big ginger tabby.

"Maybe they went to church," my mother said, probably guilty that her family had been delinquent just this once.

"Neither struck me as the church-going type," I said. "I'm sure they'll be here in a minute."

"But we agreed to all go in together," Mum fussed.

"Maybe they've gone to pick up Garth Elshaw," I said. My father went over and peered in a window.

"There's no one inside," he said. "You know, I've been here before, when it was still a church. It was a lovely one, too. Very historic. It was the first church in the Battlefords."

The date over the door was 1886.

"Built thirty years before St. Andrew's," my mother said.

"I'm surprised it's still locked," Shirley Goodman said. "It's seven minutes past 11:00, and the sign says it opens at 11:00."

"Oh, be patient," her husband said.

"It is rather bad, though," Shirley continued. "I mean, inducting us into the Hall of Fame and then keeping us cooling our heels out here like this."

"I'm sure someone will be here to open it soon," my mother said.

"I'm so excited," said Meg Deneka. "I can't remember when I've been so excited. But then I can't remember anything anyway. Can I, Peter?"

Her husband, who seemed distracted, smiled wearily.

"Where are your grandchildren?" Edna asked. "I thought they'd be here."

"They're long gone," my mother said. "They were on the road just after breakfast. Amy had a birthday party she couldn't miss, and Sheila doesn't like to be away from Buddy too long. They don't care about a bunch of dusty old bats and balls anyway."

"Now, dear," my father said. "You know they would have stayed if they could. They were here for the important part, anyway."

"Yes, wasn't that a nice evening," Edna said.

"I was just glad there was no trouble," Shirley said, "and that letter writer didn't get up to any tricks."

"Look, this is probably Virna now," Peter Deneka said, as a station wagon pulled up and parked at the curb in front of the giant baseball bats.

But it wasn't the Wiltons. I recognized Ruth Fernie, one of the volunteers from the banquet. She came up the front walk with tiny quick steps, apologizing all the while.

"With the excitement last night, we all slept in, and I've been running behind all morning. I am so sorry to have kept you waiting. What will you think of our hospitality?"

We assured her that we had not been inconvenienced.

"Mr. Shury will be very annoyed if he hears I kept Hall of Famers waiting."

We told her he wouldn't hear it from our lips.

"Well, I'll just get the key, and you can have your tour."

She bustled around the side of the building, and reappeared in a moment, holding up the key and smiling.

"Secret hiding place," she said. "Really, I don't know why we bother locking it. There's nothing worth stealing. Don't tell Mr. Shury I said that."

She unlocked the door and opened it wide.

"Shall we wait for Virna?" my mother asked.

"We agreed on eleven and it's almost a quarter past," Edna said. "I spent half my playing career waiting for Virna Wilton, and I'm not going to do it now."

She was first through the door, rolling her walker ahead of her, the rest of us following. We paused inside the door to let our eyes adjust to the shadowy room after the brightness of the morning.

"I'll just go get the lights," Mrs. Fernie said. "Maybe you could sign the guest book while you're waiting."

Shirley Goodman picked up the pen first, and had just begun to write her name when two things happened in quick succession. First, the lights went on. Then Ruth Fernie began to scream.

The sound froze us for a moment, then Andy ran towards the front of the church. I was right behind him. Ruth was standing to one side of what had been the altar, in an area that was clearly the museum's library, hands over most of her face, with only one eye peeking out. When we came to her, all she could do was point, wordlessly.

Andy stepped in front of me quickly, but not before I'd glimpsed the garish tableau. At first I thought it was one of the plastic mannequins that were posed around the museum in the uniforms of long-defunct teams. But this one, in its jaunty yellow Racine Belles outfit, was more lifelike than the others. Or, more to the point, more *death*like. Even from the brief look I got, there was no doubt in my mind why Virna hadn't made her appointment that morning.

"Get the rest of them out of here," Andy said, urgently. "Then find a phone and call the police."

I turned in time to intercept my mother coming around a display case. I grabbed her roughly by the shoulders and turned her around.

"You don't want to go back there," I said.

"Kate! What ever are you doing?" she complained.

I handed her off to Daddy.

"Take her outside," I said. "Get everybody outside and don't let them back in."

Andy helped Mrs. Fernie to the front of the museum and found a chair for her, then went back to the body.

"Is there a phone?" I asked her. She pointed to a cabinet displaying Hall of Fame souvenirs. I found the phone behind it, on a small shelf. I dialled 911, not sure if the service existed in the boonies, but it was answered immediately. I told the despatcher the situation, and she told me to stay on the line. She was back in a moment.

"There's a car on the way," she said. "How many people are on the scene?"

"There are, let's see, around ten, I think."

"It's important that no one touches anything."

"Most of them are outside," I said. "The one that's inside is a Toronto police detective. He knows about crime scenes."

I hung up and went back to join Andy.

"They're on their way."

I looked over at the organ. I could see now that Virna had been propped up into her grotesque pose at the organ, as if she was playing the thing. There was even sheet music on the stand, but I couldn't make out the title.

"What happened?

"I can't tell," he said. "I didn't want to disturb anything once I'd established that she was dead. We'll have to wait for the medical examiner."

"Where are the police? They should be here by now."

"You go on outside with the others," he said, gently.

"I don't mind," I said.

"I do. One of us with nightmares is enough."

I went outside. My mother, father, and Edna were comforting Ruth Fernie, who was in tears. The rest didn't look too hot either. The Goodmans were sitting on one of the baseball bats. I could see the Denekas in their van. I went to talk to my parents.

"The police are on their way," I said.

"Is it Virna? Is she dead?" my mother asked. "It can't be true."

"I'm afraid it is," I said, then turned to Ruth Fernie.

"Mrs. Fernie, that hidden key you used, how many people know about it?" I asked.

"Well, all the volunteers know. It's not much of a secret."

"The murderer must have known," I said. "Don't forget to mention that to the police."

I went to speak to the others. Shirley Goodman was on me with questions the moment I got within earshot.

"My God, Kate, what happened? I'm just sick."

"They don't know that yet, Mrs. Goodman. We have to wait for the police and the medical examiner."

"But you think it's murder? She didn't just have a heart attack or something?"

"This definitely wasn't natural causes," I said.

"Poor Virna," she said. "Why did it have to be her? She was just so much fun. She was so alive. And now . . ."

She burst into tears. Her husband put his arm around her.

"Does this have anything to do with those letters the women got?" he asked.

"One of us might be next on the list," she wailed, and looked around, as if expecting an attack.

I reassured her as best I could, then went over to the Denekas. Meg looked confused. Peter held her hand, stroking it.

"I don't understand," she said, querulously. "Why can't we go inside? I want to see the museum."

"Not right now, Meggie," Peter said. "We'll come back another time."

"We'll have to go in without Virna, that's all there is to it. We can't wait all day, can we?"

Her husband smiled sadly at me, then turned back to his wife.

"They won't let us in right now," he said. "There's been some sort of accident. We'll just wait here until the police come. Then we'll go to the hotel and have a nice cup of tea."

"But I want to go inside. Why won't you let me go inside?"

I turned away and started back over to my family. A car pulled up and parked behind Ruth Fernie's station wagon. I expected to see Inspector Digby, but Jack Wilton got out, smiling sheepishly, and walked over to me.

"Sorry I'm late," he said. "You should have gone ahead without me."

I stared at him stupidly. My brain seemed to have seized up.

"I've got to say I've got quite a head on me this morning," he continued, ruefully. "I didn't even come to until twenty minutes ago."

He stopped and looked closely at me.

"Is something wrong?"

Before I could answer him, we heard the sirens, coming around the corner.

Jack looked wildly around the yard.

"Where's my mother? Where is she?"

CHAPTER

14

Andy was still inside the building when the first police-men arrived on the scene, a pair of uniformed officers, one burly, one slim, both impossibly young.

"What are you doing here?" the big one asked.

"Just securing the scene and waiting for you," he said.

"You'll have to go outside," said the partner. "God knows what you've messed up."

Andy didn't bother to introduce himself, just smiled and stepped outside the door to wait for Inspector Digby.

"What's going on?" he asked Andy when he got there.

"Virna Wilton. She's dead. Probable strangulation."

"Did you touch anything?"

"I checked for signs of life, then got out of the way."

Digby nodded and grunted his approval.

"Don Deutsch is on his way with some of his people. I'm going to have to call in the medical examiner and the boys from the Identification unit. On a Sunday, no less."

He ran his hand over his brushcut wearily.

"I'm closing off the scene. Constable Resnick here will control the door." He turned to the bigger constable. "You know the drill, Dewey."

"Yes, sir. Everyone signs in and out, with time and reason for being here. No exceptions."

"And since you're just another civilian in this jurisdiction," Digby said to Andy, "I'm afraid you have no reason to be here at the moment."

"I understand."

"No offence."

"None taken. If I can be of any help, let me know."

Displaced, he left the building and came over to where I was sitting on the grass with Jack, who had his head in his hands.

"I'm sorry about your mother," Andy said, sitting beside him.

Jack looked at him blankly.

"Thank you," he said, finally.

"Can we get out of here, Andy?" I asked. "Can we go back to the hotel? These people shouldn't have to wait in the sun."

"We'll have to stay until they tell us what to do," he said.

"Is it going to take long? Poor Meg Deneka barely knows where she is."

"It will take as long as it takes. You know that, Kate."

"Maybe if you explained to them," I said.

"I'm just another witness here, remember. I'm sure they want us out of the way as much as we do. Be patient."

"Can you just tell me what happened?" Jack asked Andy.

Andy has had a lot of experience at this sort of thing, talking to victims' relatives, and he's good at it. I knew enough to get up and leave them alone. A uniformed constable stopped me when I tried to get into the hall.

"I need to speak with Inspector Digby," I said.

"You have to wait for him to come out."

A man carrying a medical bag came up.

"Morning, Dewey," he said, cheerfully. "Another Sunday shot to hell."

"Sign in, Doc. Inspector's inside."

The doctor signed a log book. The constable carefully noted the time in and the reason for the visit in the space provided. I walked back to where my parents were standing, watching the police put up crime-scene tape. There were half a dozen in uniform. Other investigators arrived carrying cameras and other crime-scene equipment. Each signed in before entering the building. The press arrived, including a film crew, but they were kept behind the yellow tape with the rest of the civilians. Half the town seemed to be there, from kids on tricycles to seniors with walkers. They gawked at us as if we were the Sunday morning entertainment.

Staff Sergeant Morris arrived, with a guy wearing a jacket and tie with jeans. I intercepted them before they got to the door.

"Sergeant Morris, I need your help," I said. He stopped.

"Please, can we get these witnesses back to the hotel? These are elderly people who have had a terrible shock."

"We'll see what we can do," Morris said, not unkindly. "It's up to Sergeant Deutsch, here, who will be in charge of the investigation. This is Kate Henry, Don. She's the daughter of one of the women ballplayers, and Inspector Munro's friend."

He gave me a glance and a perfunctory handshake.

"I'll check out the scene and get back to you," he said.

They both signed the log and disappeared inside.

I went back to Andy and Jack and sat down. Nothing was said until the thin constable approached us a few minutes later.

"Inspector Munro, Inspector Digby would like to speak with you, if you'll come with me."

Andy got up without a word and followed the constable inside the building, where he found Digby standing with Deutsch and Morris, watching the medical examiner at work on the corpse. They all shook hands.

"This is turning into a busman's holiday for you," Digby said.

"No, it's your case," Andy said. "You're welcome to it."

"As a matter of fact, we could use your help, if you don't mind."

Andy looked at the other two policemen. Morris smiled pleasantly. Deutsch looked at the ground, the muscle at the corner of his jaw working at his resentment.

"What sort of help?" Andy asked.

"I don't have to tell you that we have to work very quickly on this one," Digby said. "There are a lot of people to talk to, people who have plans to leave. We could use an extra hand, another pair of eyes and ears this afternoon, and you already know some of the women. Are you game?"

"Sure," he said. "Glad to be of help."

While Andy was being briefed, I was listening to Jack, trying, the best I could, to help him.

"She was going to call to make sure I was up in time this morning," he said, tears running down his cheeks. "I thought she had forgotten, or saw how drunk I was last night and was teaching me a lesson. Or being kind."

He wiped his eyes with the heels of his hands. His voice shook when he continued.

"She was so full of life last night. I can't believe that was the last time I'm going to see her. I can't believe she's not going to walk out of that place, laughing. Like it's all a great big joke. She loved jokes. She and Wilma were always playing practical jokes on each other."

"I know how you must feel."

He looked at me, his eyes red and bleak.

"You can't know."

I looked away.

"But thank you," he said, and took my hand. We sat that way, him holding tightly to my hand, for the next five minutes.

Finally, Andy came out with Inspector Digby, who called us all together by the door.

"There's no reason you all have to stay here," Digby said. "Inspector Munro here has agreed to supervise your getting back to the hotel. I will request that you stay there until we have a chance to interview you this afternoon."

"We were planning to check out today," Bert Goodman complained. "We have a flight out of Saskatoon in the morning."

"We will attempt to be as efficient as possible," Digby said. "There should be officers there to take your statements within the hour."

"That's fine, Inspector," Shirley Goodman said. "We don't really have to leave tomorrow."

She looked at her husband, who was about to object.

"For Pete's sake, Bert, you're retired. It's not like you have anything to rush back for."

Peter Deneka agreed to stay, as did my parents and Edna Summers.

"I won't leave until I know who did this terrible thing," she said.

"Inspector," Shirley Goodman said, "what about our safety? All of the Belles got the same crazy letters that Virna did. We could be next on the list. Are we going to have any protection?"

Digby stiffened a bit.

"We are aware of the letters," he said. "Undoubtedly, they will figure in the investigation."

"But what about us?" Shirley whined. "We need protection."

"Just stay close to the hotel," Digby said. "About the letters, if you have any with you, please turn them over to Inspector Munro, whom you can consider part of this investigation, even though he is not a member of our department."

"But what if it's one of us who did it?" Shirley said. We looked around uneasily.

"Shut up and get into the car," Bert said. "Don't you know when to keep your mouth shut?"

We nervously retraced our happier footsteps of earlier in the day back to our cars. The gawkers stepped aside to make way. The reporters rushed over to scrum Digby.

"Jack, you ride with us," my father said. "Someone else can bring your car."

"I'll do it," my mother said. Jack handed her his keys.

Edna pushed her walker slowly towards the Denekas' van. Peter walked over to us.

"I have letters," he said. "Meg doesn't even know they came. I'll get them to you as soon as we get to the hotel."

We agreed to meet in the poolside café as soon as we had straightened out our room arrangements. Then we got into the little rental car, which had been parked in the sun. We rolled down the windows and turned on the fan, which wasn't much help.

"What happens now?" I asked as we turned towards the highway.

"Right now, I have to set up an interview room. Digby says the hotel's got a conference room they'll let us use. Then it's just the usual drill. This case is more complicated than some, because it involves so many potential witnesses, especially ones from out of town. We'll get basic statements from everyone who was at the dinner last night. And home addresses so we can contact them later if needed. If I was in charge of the investigation, which I'm not, I would concentrate on her team-mates, the ones who saw the most of her in the past few days."

"She was with a bunch in the bar last night," I said.

"I know. Can you put together a list?"

"I'll check with my mother, or Edna. They can help with the ones I don't know."

"Get it to me as soon as you can. Especially the ones who stayed until the end."

"Yeah. I didn't notice, but I think Edna hung in, anyway."

We turned into the parking lot.

"Do you mind getting involved?" I asked him.

"I don't mind it half as much as Donald Deutsch does."

"It's like that, is it? You'll have to use your famous tact, then."

"I think I forgot to bring it on this trip."

"Well, you were good with Jack back there."

He turned off the engine.

"Well, I'm not a complete asshole. Not all the time, anyway."

"Relatively seldom, if you must know."

We got out of the car.

"But when you are," I said, "you take all the prizes."

CHAPTER

15

I intercepted my mother and Edna in the lobby, and explained about Andy's need for the list of women who had been at the post-banquet party.

"If you can," I said, "he wants to know who was there until the end and who left early."

"I was one of the first to go," my mother said.

"Don't worry, Helen, I was one of the last," Edna said. "Virna and I left at the same time."

"I think this is urgent," I said. "And confidential."

"We'll do it in my room, right away," Edna said.

"Thanks. I'll tell Daddy where you are."

I went outside and lit a smoke while I waited for my father and Jack to arrive. A pickup truck pulled up near the hotel entrance where I stood and Garth Elshaw and Morley Timms got out.

"Is it true?" Morley asked. "About Virna?"

"I'm afraid so," I said, then introduced myself to Garth

Elshaw. He was dressed in work pants and a worn cotton shirt. He held a baseball cap in his hands. I was struck by his size and his dignity.

"How did it happen?" he asked.

I told him what little I knew.

"The police will be along to talk with anyone who saw her in the past few days," I said.

Morley Timms was looking over my shoulder, twisting his round-brimmed sun hat in his big freckled hands. I turned and saw Jack and my father.

Timms stepped out to meet them.

"My condolences for the loss of your mother," he said, formally, to Jack, who thanked him.

"It wasn't her time yet," Timms continued. "She was a woman in the prime of her life. It's a terrible thing."

He began to cry. Garth Elshaw stepped between his friend and Jack.

"Don't mind Morley," he said, softly. "He means well."

"Why don't we go inside," I said. "No point standing out in the sun."

Everyone turned towards the door, letting Jack go first. He went to the elevator. My father stepped up to him.

"Would you like me to come with you? Sometimes it helps to talk."

"I just want to be alone for a while. I should make some calls, too. But thank you."

My father put his hand on Jack's shoulder.

"I'll check on you in a little while."

"Thank you."

He stepped into the elevator, looking bleak and broken. The door closed.

"He's pretty cut up," Garth said.

"He's had a bad blow," Morley Timms said. He turned his hat in his hands, around and around, his fingers jittering at the brim. "It puts me in mind of some of the fellows during the war. Shell-shocked, we called it. Even strong young men. We saw our share, didn't we, Garth?"

"I don't think they want to hear about it, Morley," he said.

"He was very close to his mother," I said, thinking of our conversation of the night before. "And of course, he loved your sister, too. It's as if he's lost two mothers in six months. That would be hard for anyone."

"He knew Wilma better than I did, at the end," Elshaw said, with an undercurrent I couldn't quite define. Bitterness? Or just sadness?

"Well, let's not stand around out here," my father said, briskly, breaking the tension. "I think a cup of coffee might be helpful to us all."

"Good idea," I said. "I have to go to the room for a minute, and then I'll join you."

I went and used the washroom, and was heading back down the stairs when I ran into Andy.

"Have you got things set up?" I asked.

"They've given us the conference room on the second floor for whatever we need. I've ordered the coffee."

"What about donuts?" I asked. "Can't have an investigation without donuts. Or do Mounties go for muffins?"

"You know their motto," he said. "They always get their bran."

I groaned.

"I'm on the way to the café by the pool," I said. "That's where most of the people are. I don't think anyone wants to be alone."

"Given the situation, I think that's for the best. I don't want anyone who received one of those letters on her own right now."

"Jack's gone to his room. He said he had to make some calls."

"I'll check in with him."

"Daddy's keeping an eye on him, too."

We were in the lobby by then, and were joined by Edna and my mother, who handed Andy a piece of paper.

"These are the women who were in the bar. We've put ticks next to the names of the ones who were there until the end. And which one played with Virna on the Belles, or later, for the Fort Wayne Daisies. The ones we know about, anyway."

Andy took it and looked at it.

"Good work," he said. "Thanks."

Edna was looking very upset.

"It was such a good time last night," she said. "Just a bunch of gals talking about old times and laughing. You don't think someone at that table killed her, do you?"

"Not necessarily, but the police want to talk to the last people who saw her alive," Andy said.

"We weren't the last people," Edna said.

"What do you mean?" I asked.

"The murderer was," she said.

Andy and I exchanged a quick look.

"One of us could be the murderer, Edna," my mother said. "Don't you see what it looks like? We all get together for the first time in more than forty years, and this happens. It could go back to when we knew each other before."

"But why?" Edna asked. "She didn't have enemies back then, that I know of. She was popular. She was the biggest star in the league."

"What about jealousy?" I asked. "Because she got all the attention."

"No one is going to kill her after all these years just because she got on the cover of *Life* magazine," Edna said.

Andy held up the list they'd made.

"Someone here might have the answer," he said.

My mother changed the subject by asking me about my father's whereabouts.

"He's in the café by the pool," I said.

"That's where we will go, then," she said. "Come along, Edna, we must let Andy do his work."

"I almost forgot," Edna said, opening her purse.

She handed a familiar-looking envelope to Andy, who took it and gingerly pulled out the letter.

"It looks like the same handwriting," he said.

"Same different-colour inks? Same underlining?"

"Some of the same phrases," he said, showing me. "Is this the only one you got?"

"Yes, just last week," Edna said. "Do you think it's connected?"

"We certainly can't rule it out."

"I can't believe someone I know could have written this," Edna said, "let alone killed Virna."

"You'd be surprised," I said. "I've met several perfectly pleasant murderers in my day."

"Yes, Kate attracts murderers the way other people attract mosquitoes," Andy said.

"He's exaggerating," I said.

"That's why I hang out with her," Andy continued. "She makes sure I'll never be out of work."

"Cops have a strange sense of humour," I explained after he left.

CHAPTER

16

The café was full. Not only with the former Belles and their families, but with many of the other women, too. News of Virna's death had spread. There was a palpable sense of shock and gloom in the room. Those who were talking did so in lowered voices. My father was across the room, sitting with Morley Timms and Garth Elshaw. He waved when he saw us.

"I'll just go and speak with some of the other girls," Edna said.

My mother and I went to my father. I signalled a passing waitress, who brought us coffee.

"I've just been talking to Mr. Elshaw about his sister, Wilma," my father said.

"Did she come back to Battleford often?" I asked.

"Not hardly at all," he said. He had a deliberate way of speaking, with great pauses between sentences. "She came in the summers sometimes. Her and Virna, when Jack was a boy. But once he grew up, they didn't come. I hadn't seen him in more than thirty years until yesterday."

"Not at your sister's funeral?"

"Didn't go."

The way he said it told me not to pursue the subject, so I back-tracked.

"What was Jack like as a boy?"

"He was a quiet one," he said, after thinking for a few moments. "He didn't raise heck like my wife's two boys. They was always a bit rough for him. But he liked it on the farm all right, Jack did. He didn't mind doing chores."

"Garth taught him how to hunt and fish and the like, up at the cabin," Timms added.

"The boy never had a father, so I did what I could for him."

"That was nice of you," my mother said. "I'm sure he appreciated it."

"If it made any difference, I'm glad. But if it did, he forgot about it after."

"He never even got a card at Christmas," Timms said, indignant on his pal's behalf.

"So you lost touch," I said.

"After my wife passed, I invited Wilma to come home," Elshaw said, "but she wanted to stay down there in the States."

"And when she died, they had her cremated in Fort Wayne," Morley Timms added. "Instead of buried in the family plot right here in Battleford. That's not right."

"It was Wilma's wishes," Elshaw said, quietly.

"Doesn't make it right. You said so at the time," he said, then turned to me. "They didn't even have a proper

113

funeral in a church. They had something called a celebration of her life, then Virna and Jack scattered her ashes at the ballpark. At the ballpark! Have you ever heard of such a thing?"

"Let's just drop the subject," Elshaw said.

"Still say it wasn't right," Timms muttered.

We sat in silence for a few minutes.

"How did you two find out about the murder?" I asked.

"Morley heard it on the radio and came by," Elshaw said. "I was waiting on Virna and Jack to go to the museum."

"We drove by there first, but it was just the RCM Police and a bunch of fools who had nothing better to do than stare at them," Timms said. "So we just came on over here. Figured someone here would know what happened."

My mother looked at her watch.

"It's almost one," she fretted. "I wonder where the police are."

"There's always a lot more to do at a crime scene than you think," I said. "They have to take photographs and look for fingerprints and fibres and other evidence before they even take the body away."

"You know a lot about it," Timms said. "I guess because the boyfriend is a policeman."

"I read a lot of crime novels," I shrugged. "Andy doesn't talk about his work. But I'm a naturally curious person. That's why I'm a good reporter. Anytime I'm around a crime scene, I watch and learn as much as I can. Who knows? Maybe I'll get tired of covering baseball and become a crime reporter someday."

114

"That's not fit work for a woman," Timms said, shaking his round head. I smiled.

"Crime and death, that's men's business," he continued. "You should leave that alone. You wouldn't have the stomach for it."

"You'd be surprised what women's stomachs can take these days," I said.

"Mr. Timms, I suggest that you're treading on dangerous ground," my father said, mildly. "I learned long ago not to tell Kate what to do."

"He's a bit old-fashioned," Elshaw said.

"Nothing old-fashioned about good moral values," Timms went on. "When plain decency and common sense go out of fashion, that's the day you can dig that hole and plant me in it."

"I'm all for common sense, too," I said. "And politeness. Especially politeness."

Timms beamed.

"See, now. Me and Miss Henry get along just fine. We're kindred spirits."

"You bet, Mr. Timms," I said.

"What did you do for a living?" my mother asked. "I guess you're retired now. Did you farm?"

"No, I'm not retired," he said. "I'm busy all the time."

"What is it you do?"

"Most anything. Odd job man. Mr. Fix-it. That's me. I never really took to farming. I have to be my own boss. I work when I want to and there's no one to tie me down. Of course, the government pays me, too. For what I did in the war."

"I see," I said, not seeing.

"Every month, they send me a cheque. It doesn't make me rich, but I get by."

"It's the disability pay," Elshaw explained. "He's been getting it for fifty years."

"And you said last night that you never married?" I asked.

"Like I said, I never wanted to be tied down."

"So you're just the happy bachelor?"

"Footloose and fancy free," he said, with a loopy grin. "And Garth, here, he's the merry widower."

"You make quite the pair, then," I laughed. Timms joined in. Elshaw didn't.

"Have you been friends for a long time, then?" my father asked.

"Practically from birth," Timms said. "We went to school together. Played ball together. When the war came, we joined up and served together."

"In what branch?"

"Don't laugh, now," Timms said. "We were in the navy."

"Why should I laugh at that?" I asked.

"A couple of prairie boys who'd never even seen an ocean before," Elshaw said. "Some thought it was strange."

"I'd say it was pretty adventurous," I said.

"That's what we thought at the time," Elshaw said, his eyes going cold. "Some adventure it turned out to be."

"At least we made it home," Timms said.

"Yes, we made it home," Elshaw agreed. "Some didn't."

Silence fell at the table. I looked around and noticed the thin Mountie from that morning standing at the door. When he saw me, he came and introduced himself as Constable Louis Tremblay.

"Ms. Henry, would you come with me, please?"

116

CHAPTER

17

Constable Tremblay took me to the second-floor board-room and led me into a big room with a blonde oak table in the middle, covered with papers, Styrofoam cups, and muffin crumbs. Inoffensive paintings of prairie scenes hung on the walls. There were ten chairs arranged around the table, four of them occupied.

"Sit down, please," said Sergeant Deutsch, strangely formal. "As you know, as head of the General Investigation Section, I'm in charge of the investigation into the death of Virna Wilton."

As he spoke, a constable next to him turned to a fresh page in his notebook. It was the same guy who had been in charge of the log at the crime scene.

"Constable Resnick will be taking notes. Corporal Hugh Grenfell is my senior investigator. And, of course, you know Inspector Munro, who will be sitting in."

Andy winked at me. I stifled a smile.

"There are various reasons we want to talk to you," Deutsch said. "The first is, obviously, your family connection. Second, you were there at the crime scene. You have been talking to some of the women, and Inspector Munro tells me that you are a good observer. He also tells me that you have formed a relationship with the victim's son, and we would like to talk about that, too. Is there anything you would like to ask before we get started?"

I glanced at Andy. He gave me a barely perceptible shake of the head, hardly more than a twitch. I figured the signal was so subtle I could ignore it.

"How did she die?" I asked. "I didn't see any blood."

"We'll know more after the autopsy. The body is on the way to the pathologist in Saskatoon."

"But what's your gut feeling?"

Deutsch gave me a faint smile.

"Gut feelings aren't evidence, as you know, Ms. Henry. But we're not ruling out strangulation."

"Can you tell where she died?"

Andy gave me a shut-up look, which I ignored.

"I mean, if she died somewhere else, it would take someone strong to get the body here," I said. "Wouldn't that rule out most of the women?"

"I don't know," Deutsch said, amusement flashing in his eyes. "Some of those little old ladies aren't so little, or so old, either. There are a couple of them I wouldn't care to take on at arm-wrestling. I think it's fair to say that the field of suspects is wide open."

"Well, I can account for my whereabouts," I joked.

"If she says she was with me, I'm afraid I can't testify," Andy said. "I was asleep at the time."

Oh, weren't they just having fun? They had obviously already decided how to humour me.

"All right, I give up," I said. "Ask your questions."

Over the next hour, Deutsch led me back over the events of the past few days, from the arrival of the threatening letter at Indian Head to Ruth Fernie's scream. He was a good interrogator, leading me along gently but firmly, stopping me from time to time with probing questions that made me remember things I had forgotten. I was impressed. After taking me through my conversation with Virna's son for a second time, he was apparently satisfied.

"Anyone else have something?" he asked. Both Andy and Corporal Grenfell shook their heads.

"Thank you, Ms. Henry," Deutsch said. "You have been extremely helpful."

"Fingerprints," Grenfell said.

"Oh, yes," Deutsch said. "All evidence is being sent to the RCMP Forensic Laboratory in Regina, and they will need a set of prints from you for comparison with those on the letters and at the crime scene. Constable Tremblay will do the honours as you leave. Thank you once again for your cooperation."

I got up and went into the hall. While Constable Tremblay did his thing with the ink-pad and fingerprint card, I heard laughter from behind the closed meeting-room door. Three guesses who they were laughing at. Tremblay gave me a tissue which was pretty much useless at cleaning the ink off, and sent me on my way.

I thought of going to Jack's room, but decided not to disturb him, in case he had managed to sleep. In fact, I didn't feel comfortable going to his room after

Deutsch's remark about our "forming a relationship." He would be up soon on the interview list, and I didn't want to be accused of tampering or something. Instead, I went to our room to scrub my hands, then rejoined the bunch by the pool.

Garth Elshaw and Morley Timms had left, and their places at the table were taken by the Goodmans. The table was littered with lunch dishes, and I realized I was starving. It was almost three, and all I'd had for breakfast was coffee. I sat down and picked at some leftover French fries from my mother's plate.

"Where have you been?" she asked.

"Talking with the police."

"What did they ask you?"

"I'm not supposed to talk about it, I don't think. It was just general stuff. Who said what, when. Who I saw with Virna in the bar. What about the threatening letters, stuff like that. They're trying to talk to as many people as possible before everybody leaves."

"Well, we're not going anywhere," my father said. "I've arranged to stay on. They have given us a special discount. We'll just call it a holiday."

"Some holiday," Shirley Goodman said. "Trapped in this hotel wondering who's going to be next."

"We just have to be careful," my father said. "No one should go anywhere alone."

I looked around.

"Where's Edna?" I asked.

"The police just came for her," Shirley Goodman said. "It's her turn. Then it's mine."

"Well, she's here alone, so we had better watch out for her," I said.

"Of course we will, dear," my mother said.

"If you're not next to be interviewed, you should go lie down for a while," I suggested.

"Kate, I'm just old. I'm not an invalid," my mother said.

"I didn't say you were."

"I'm not feeble," she grumbled.

"All I'm saying is that it's been a tough day," I said. "I'm probably going to lie down myself. Forget I said anything."

"I'm sorry," she said. "I'm just feeling a bit strained. I shouldn't have taken it out on you."

"We're all under stress," Shirley Goodman said. "And it's no wonder. There's some madman out there with a grudge and the police can't do anything about it."

"If only they had taken those letters seriously, this might never have happened," my mother said.

"Or if Virna had taken it seriously," Shirley Goodman said.

"That was never her style," my mother said. "She was always one to take risks."

"How's her son?" Shirley Goodman asked.

"He's shaken up, obviously," I said. "He's gone to his room to make some phone calls."

"I think I'll go and see if he wants anything," my father said. "I told him I would, and he might like some company. Will you come, too, Helen?"

"No. Go without me. I'm going to take Kate's advice and lie down for a little while."

"Do you think you should be alone?" Shirley Goodman asked.

"I won't open my door to anyone," she said.

"We'll come up with you, then, and make sure you get to your room all right," Shirley Goodman said.

"I don't think that's necessary," my mother said.

"Better safe than sorry," Shirley Goodman said.

CHAPTER

18

After my parents and the Goodmans left, I looked around for company and saw the Denekas across the room. They seemed happy to have me join them. I ordered a grilled cheese sandwich and ate it while we talked.

"You look so much like your mother did," Mrs. Deneka said. "You're older than she was when we played baseball, of course. But you have the same curly hair. She was quite a beauty, you know. She broke a lot of hearts. I bet you have, too."

"I'm afraid it's been the other way around," I said.

"Never mind. You have a nice young man now," she said.

"Thank you. I'm afraid I've lost him for the moment, though. He's busy being a policeman."

"Oh, well, it gives the rest of us a chance to visit."

"Yes, it's wonderful to meet all my mother's old friends," I said. "And to find out about the league, too. My mother hardly ever talks about it. She says she doesn't remember."

"Well, dear, it's different for me," she said, with a little smile. "I remember it as if it were yesterday."

"You remember it better than yesterday," Peter teased, and was rewarded by a smile from his wife.

"Well, that's just the way my brain works now," she said to me. "I may have a few screws loose, but I don't let it worry me, or else I'd turn into a sad old lady."

"Never you, Meggie," her husband said. "Besides, I like it that you think of me as the handsome young man I once was."

"Yes, except when I wonder who that old goat is who wants to get into bed with me."

I laughed, astonished. Meg put her hands over her mouth like a naughty girl. Peter grinned. They were a pair.

"Last night you called my father Carl," I said. "Tell me why. Was there a Carl in Mum's life then?"

"Well, I don't want to tell tales," she said.

"It's too late for that," her husband said.

"It was a long time ago, remember. Before she met your father. Yes, Carl was her beau. He was a big, handsome boy. He was of Norwegian stock from right there in Racine. There are a lot of Norwegians in Wisconsin. He wasn't blond, though, like so many of them. I can't remember his last name. Jorgenson, Johannsen, one of those names. Anyway, he sure was stuck on your mother, and she was fond of him, too. I wonder what happened to him?"

"Did all the girls have boyfriends?"

"Let's just say there were always plenty of boys waiting outside the stadium. And they weren't looking for batting tips."

"But I thought you were strictly controlled. Didn't you have curfews and chaperones?"

"Of course. That was part of the fun, sneaking past them."

"How?"

"Some of the girls were very good at climbing out of boarding-house windows, I can tell you that much. Of course, I didn't go in for that kind of thing. I had my sweetheart at home."

"You?" I asked Peter Deneka.

"Me," he said. "I was back on the farm, waiting for the postman."

"We wrote each other every day," Meg explained. "Even when he was overseas."

"I guess a lot of the girls in the league had people in the service," I said.

"Oh my, yes. Every time the Western Union boy came, it would throw terror into all our hearts. Terror. I lost my baby brother. Poor Virna lost her husband. And there were others, too."

"When was it that Virna's husband died?"

"I don't exactly remember. It happened over the win-ter, I know, because when she came to spring training, with her little baby, she told us. That was little Johnny, we called him. Of course he's Jack, now. Hasn't he grown up to be a handsome lad?"

"Yes, he has," I said. "Was Virna a good mother, or did he cramp her style? I guess she must have been a pretty wild one."

"No, not really. Virna could be a little madcap, but she was all business when it came to baseball. It was her life, and after baseball, it was Johnny. She was devoted to him. Absolutely devoted. We all were. He was such a little angel."

"How did she take care of him with the team travelling?"

"Oh, she just brought him along. She was our biggest star, so she could do whatever she wanted. When he didn't come along, he stayed at home with her landlady. I guess she paid a little extra. Or, probably, the league paid for it. I don't guess I ever knew about that."

"Who was her husband? Did you know him?"

"I don't recall him. I think she got married in the winter between the first and second seasons. I remember being surprised when she told us she was married, so I don't suppose I ever met him. He was from Davidson, she said, her high school sweetheart. I remember that. He went overseas that year, 1944, and died the next winter. Yes, that was it, because I remember now that Johnny was just a tiny baby when the war ended, in 1945."

"And afterwards? Did she date?"

"Like I said, she was all baseball and that baby. Not that there wasn't interest. Even now you could see she was a beauty."

"Yes, she was," I said.

"Although I do remember a fellow one time, so handsome in his Royal Canadian Navy uniform. Or was that Wilma's beau? I get confused."

She smiled at me, apologetically.

"You're doing very well," I said.

"If I only did so well with things that happened last week, I'd be fine."

She laughed, a warm, contagious sound.

"Were you in the league right from the beginning?" I asked.

"Your mother and Virna and I were, yes. Edna came the next year, 1944, along with Wilma. Shirley, or Rosie as we called her then, came in 1945. That's when the team really came together."

"The year the war ended."

"Yes. And we won the championship the next year. Did you ever meet Wilma Elshaw?"

"No, I never did."

"She was a beautiful player. She ran like a deer, could catch anything hit to centre field, and she had an arm like a gun. And she could hit, too. She averaged over .300 every year. She was a treat to play with."

Her recall of fifty years ago was sharp and true. As she reminisced, she reminded me of old major leaguers, coaches, and scouts I have talked to who can remember exact details of games played in the thirties, down to the exact pitch hit, and what the count was at the time. It's something about the baseball mind, I guess. Or the ego of an athlete.

After a while, she began to tire, and drifted more and more into her reveries. I could see that it was pointless to ask her any more questions. I smiled at Peter Deneka.

"I've taken up too much of your time," I said. "You'll want to rest up before talking with the police. Maybe we can get together later this evening."

"Yes, dear. Let's stick together," she said, then sang: "We're all for one, we're one for all."

"We're All-American," I said.

"You bet."

CHAPTER

19

My message light was flashing when I got back to my room just before four: Edna Summers. I called and invited myself to her room.

"What did the police tell you?" she asked, when I got there.

"Nothing much. They're a close-mouthed bunch. I hope I can get more out of Andy when he's done tonight."

"Oh, pillow talk," she winked.

"I guess," I said, thinking that we hadn't been doing much of that in the last few days, or much of anything else on pillows, for that matter.

"I was just talking with Peter and Meg Deneka," I went on. "She's an awfully nice woman, isn't she?"

"Yes. Too bad she's talking to the birdies these days," Edna said, briskly. "Her body hasn't suffered the way mine has, or Rosie Goodman's, but at least we've still got our minds. Meg was smart as a whip when she was younger. She was a real card, too. She used to keep us in stitches. She and Virna were a pair. They'd work up little skits for the bus rides and organize shows for the end-of-season banquets. Meg would sing and dance and Virna would do impressions. She could imitate anybody – the chaperones, other players, the owners, even the league president. She was doing it last night when we were all together in the bar. I thought I'd wet my pants, I was laughing so hard."

She stopped, then sighed.

"Oh, that seems like a long time ago, doesn't it? It wasn't even twenty-four hours ago we were all having so much fun."

"I know. It's hard to imagine."

"It just makes me so darn mad," she said. "If we had taken those letters seriously, this would never have happened. She wouldn't have gone off with whoever it was."

"Well, we can't know that. It must have been someone she knew, someone she trusted."

"I wonder. Do you think it happened last night, or this morning?"

"Because of the way she was dressed, I would guess last night."

"Oh, but that might have been part of the prank," Edna said, almost to herself.

"What do you mean?"

"I'd forgotten until just now," Edna said, "but last night, some of the girls were talking about sneaking into the Hall of Fame and playing some sort of joke."

"Who?"

"It was Elsie Stiegler and Dodie Nowland, two of the girls who played for the Daisies, who came up with the idea. But no one knew how to get in, so they dropped it."

"What were they going to do?"

"I'm not sure. I wasn't in on that part of the conversation."

"But if Virna found a way to get in, she might have gone there to set something up. Did you tell the police about that part of the conversation?"

"No, I just now remembered it."

"We'd better go tell them."

We went down to the second floor, where we found the conference room shut, but Constable Tremblay said he would deliver a message.

"We'll be in the bar," Edna said. I looked at my watch.

"It's not even five yet," I said.

She shrugged.

"With the time difference, it's happy hour in Toronto."

"It's always happy hour somewhere," I said.

"You've just got to worry when you start celebrating it in Newfoundland," she said.

The bar was empty, and quieter than it had been the night before, but it was still pretty raunchy. We sat against the wall farthest from the bar. The bartender called across to us and asked what we wanted, then brought Edna a rye and Seven and a beer for me.

"Cheers," I said, raising my glass. "To happier days."

"To the All-American Girls Professional Baseball League."

"It sounds like you had lots of fun."

"We surely did, but that's not all. We played good baseball, too. We drew good crowds."

"Well, yeah, but it was wartime, right?"

"You mean we got the crowds because we were the only game in town?" she asked, indignantly. "Shame on you. A woman sportswriter not knowing anything about our league."

She was right. I was as locked in as any male sportswriter to the myth that only big league sports are interesting, and big league sports are played by men. If I had thought about the All-American Girls at all, I thought of it as glorified softball. Hey, how serious could it have been? My *mother* played in it.

"You're right, you know. I should write a feature story for my paper about you all and the induction. I'll call my editor in the morning."

"But the girls are all leaving."

"You're not, Edna. I'll make you the star of the piece."

"Well, that would be a first."

"We'll start right now," I said. "How did you get involved in the league?"

"I was a tomboy in Watrous, wanting to play baseball while all my friends were growing up and getting married. I felt like some sort of freak. Then I saw the story in *Life* magazine about the All-American Girls, the one with Virna on the cover, and wrote a letter to the league president. He told me about the try-out camp in Chicago. It took all my savings to get there, but I got accepted for the 1944 season."

"What did your family think about it?"

"Oh, my, they were dead set against it," she said. "They wanted me to go on with my education, or else settle down and get married."

"But you went anyway?"

"I went anyway. The first time I ever defied them. In the end, they accepted it. When I became an all-star, my father's friends all began to congratulate him. But my mother wasn't happy until I quit."

"You were all so brave back then," I said. "I can't imagine what it must have been like."

"Why not? You've broken ground in your job, too."

"Being the first woman in the press box doesn't exactly rank with Jackie Robinson in baseball history," I said. "Or with you women doing what you did during the war. That took courage. What I do just needs a thick skin."

"Well, I admire you."

"Thank you, Edna. I wish my mother was more like you."

"Don't be silly. She's very proud of you."

"Did she tell you that?"

"She didn't have to. I can see it in her face."

"Maybe you're right. But she doesn't approve of where the job takes me – like into the locker room."

Edna giggled.

"She's probably jealous. I know I am. All those naked young men."

"It's less interesting than you think," I said.

"Well, I wouldn't mind taking a peek."

"A peek at what?"

I looked up. Andy was standing beside the table.

"Edna wants to go into the locker room with me," I said. Andy smiled.

"I'm shocked," he said.

"But not surprised?"

"Nothing about you surprises me, Edna."

20

Edna told Andy about Virna and the Daisies wanting to play a practical joke.

"Interesting," he said. "So someone with a key might have brought her there."

"But no one had a key last night," Edna said.

"It must have been common knowledge among the people connected with the museum," I said. "Remember that Ruth Fernie got it from its hiding place this morning."

"It's worth looking into," Andy said. "Thanks."

"Are you done for the day?" I asked him.

"Afraid not. We're just taking a break between interviews."

"Who did you just talk with?"

"Jack Wilton. Next we're talking to the Denekas. Although I'm not sure how much help she'll be."

"And my parents? They'll want to be getting to their supper, you know."

"Got it covered already. We're doing them after supper."

"When are you going to eat? I'll wait for you."

"I'll check back with you after the next interview."

After he left, I turned to Edna.

"I should probably go talk to them," I said.

"Let me tell you about some things I found out this afternoon, first," Edna said.

"What?"

"I talked with some of the girls who played with Virna in Fort Wayne. One of them, Elsie Stiegler, still has friends there, and says that there was a lot of talk at the time of Wilma's death."

She gave me a significant look.

"What kind of talk?"

"That it wasn't exactly on the up and up. That she died sooner than she was expected to."

"That she was helped along?"

"Exactly."

"By Virna?"

"And Jack. No charges were laid, but like I said, some think it was fishy."

"Did you tell this to the police?"

"Oh, yes, and that's not all Elsie told me. She and her husband, Ned, moved to Davidson, Virna's home town, after Ned retired, and they got to know some people who knew Virna when she was young. It seems that people there were surprised when she had that baby, too. They didn't even know she was married."

"But I thought she married someone from home. That's what Meg Deneka said."

"That's what Virna told us at the time. She said she went home over the winter and came back married."

"And he died the next winter, didn't he?"

"Yes, just before she had the baby."

"That was either very tragic or very convenient," I said. "And none of you ever met him?"

"No, we didn't. To tell the truth, dear, some of us thought it was passing strange at the time, because Virna sure didn't seem like the marrying kind, if you know what I mean."

She gave me a look, a nudge-nudge-wink-wink kind of look.

"But in that case, if I know what you mean, she would hardly be the getting pregnant kind either."

"Well, life's full of little secrets," Edna said. "And if Virna wanted a child badly enough, there were ways, even then."

"But the timing seems strange, right at the height of her career. Oh well, I doubt it had anything to do with her death."

"I guess not," Edna said, sounding disappointed. "It's probably something else entirely. Something dull. Like on TV, it's usually someone in the family that does the murder. To inherit the money."

"Jack? I don't think so," I said. "For one thing, I was with him last night after his mother went to bed, and believe me, he was in no shape to murder anyone."

"I remember once on 'Murder She Wrote', there was the same situation. But Jessica Fletcher discovered that the killer had been drinking water all night, not martinis."

"Well, Jack was drinking Scotch," I said. "And I saw the bartender pour it out of the bottle. Unless, of course, the bartender was in on the conspiracy and the bottle was full of iced tea. But I doubt it. Besides, he really loved

Virna. I could tell by the way he talked about her, and by seeing them together."

"Oh, well," she said, then leaned in close to me. "Don't look now, but here he comes."

I looked up, feeling faintly guilty to be talking about him behind his back.

"Mind if I join you?"

"Of course not," I said.

He sat heavily in a chair.

"I've just come from the police. They don't seem to know very much."

"Well, it's early yet," I said, feeling some strange need to defend them. Loyalty to Andy, I guess.

"They gave me a pretty good going-over," he said. "I think I'm lucky I was with you last night."

Edna darted a glance in my direction.

"Oh, God, none of this makes any sense," he said. "I can't figure out why this happened. Was it someone she knew? Did someone hate her that much? Someone carrying a grudge for all these years? I can't get my head around it."

"I can't believe that any of the girls are involved," Edna said.

"But there has to be some connection," he said. "Why else would she have been killed in the Hall of Fame?"

Edna told him about her wanting to go to the Hall of Fame to pull off a practical joke.

"That sounds like her," he said, smiling sadly.

"But no one knew where to get a key, so they dropped the idea," Edna said. "Besides, it was almost one in the morning by the time we left."

"That doesn't mean anything," Jack said. "My mother was a night owl."

"Virna always would go to any length to pull off one of her pranks," Edna said.

"Well, then it means her murderer had to be in the bar last night," I said.

"I say it was someone local," Edna said. "Remember, the letters were postmarked from here."

I could sense Jack's discomfort, and tried to change the subject.

"Look, this isn't getting us anywhere. Let's just leave it to the police."

"You're right, Kate," Edna said. "In fact, I'm going to leave you two and see if I can find someone to have supper with."

"My parents should be ready right about now," I said.

"And I'll tell them that you're waiting for Andy," she said, getting up.

"Thanks."

Jack and I sat in silence for a few moments after she left. I couldn't think of anything to say that wasn't either morbid or inappropriate.

"How are you feeling?" was what I finally came up with.

"Not so hot," he said. "I spent the afternoon just thinking about her, wishing I'd had a chance to say goodbye. Regretting things I had said to her over the years, or things I didn't say and wish I had."

"I'm sure she knew," I said.

"I hope you're right."

"You got along so well, how could she not know?"

"Well, we weren't always that close. In fact, things were pretty rocky for a while when I was younger. I had a lot of anger in me."

"What about?"

"You can guess, can't you?" he asked. "Growing up the way I did. I had a couple of years in my teens when I spent half my time fighting with other kids. This was after they figured out that dykes weren't just sea walls in Holland.

"I'd come home all bloody and they would want to know why, but I was too ashamed to tell them. I'd make up a story and then go out and do it all over again."

"Why didn't you just tell her?"

"In 1957? It wasn't exactly something a boy could talk to his mother about. So, finally, I went to the phys ed teacher at school, Coach Newman, and asked him to teach me to fight."

"And?"

"They stopped bothering me after a while."

"Did you ever talk to your mother about it?"

"I tried. But she just got mad at people who wouldn't mind their own business. I was really angry about it for a while there. I really hated her."

He ordered another drink.

"Look, I don't even know what went on between them. I didn't want to know. Lots of unmarried women lived together. That didn't have to mean anything. It's not as if they walked around holding hands or anything. They slept in separate rooms. But I couldn't explain that to anyone. Anyway, my friends stopped coming around, so I stayed out more and more."

Through it all, he said, his mother and Wilma Elshaw had tried to teach him to judge a person by who he or she is, not by what people say, and that small-minded people should be ignored. Good advice maybe, but not easy for an adolescent to take. It had taken him years to come through the confusion and anger, finally, but he had ended up with a strong and protective bond with his mother and his "Aunt Wilma."

"I was devastated when Wilma died," he said. "I'm still trying to come to grips with it. It was very sudden, just three months between diagnosis and when she passed on. And now my mother's gone, too."

"I wish there was something I could say."

"You've helped just by listening," he said.

CHAPTER

21

Later, in bed, I tried to get Andy to talk about the case.

"No meddling, in this one," he said. "It's too danger-ous."

"I don't meddle."

"Of course you do. Meddling is your favourite recreation. It's your prime hobby. It's your avocation. It's practically your religion."

Our disagreement over my curiosity and the trouble it gets me into is one we'll never resolve. But it's not a fight either of us takes seriously. It has just become part of who we are, together. Andy always ends up telling me what I want to know eventually, so I dropped it for the moment and enjoyed being with him. It's a lovely form of intima-cy, lying in the dark, talking, until the silences take over and we drift away. I wasn't ready for that yet, though.

"Talk about meddling, Edna's sticking both her oars into everything, isn't she?"

"I'm not sure that Deutsch and the other horsemen appreciate her," Andy said. "But I do."

"How come when she does it it's okay, and when I do it it's meddling?"

"Because she's harmless, and you're not. And I don't worry about her getting herself into trouble the way you usually do."

"Don't fall for that little old lady stuff," I said. "And you should worry about her. Don't forget she got letters too."

"We've put the fear of God in her about wandering away from the safety of the hotel. And I've told her to report everything she hears to you. That should keep you both out of trouble."

He snickered. I took advantage of his expansive mood.

"What do you think of the investigation so far?"

"It's by the book," he said. "A little uninspired, but certainly thorough. Deutsch has got a bit of a chip on his shoulder about big-city cops, but that's to be expected. I've got my own feelings about the Mounties, for that matter. But we're feeling each other out gradually."

"Cop-bonding over a couple of drinks?"

"It's going to work out fine. I think he's a good cop."

"He did a good interview with me," I agreed. "And he was smart enough to involve you."

"That was Digby's doing. But Deutsch can see that my social connection with the victim's friends can be useful. I did the interview with your mother, for example."

"What did she have to offer?"

"She seemed uncomfortable, at first," he said. "Probably because she was seeing me in action as a cop for the first time instead of as her daughter's beau."

"Beau?"

"Whatever. Anyway, she relaxed eventually. She's got a good eye. I can see where you got it from."

"I don't think I got much from my mother," I said. "My curly hair, and my love of baseball, that's about it."

"Are you crazy? You're just like her. You look like her, you sound like her. You insist on folding the damn towels the way she does it."

"No, I'm like my dad. Sheila's like my mum. She's the one who's Mrs. Perfect, not me."

"You're rigid in your judgements of people, just like she is," Andy continued.

"I am not. I'm not a prude. I don't go around condemning people for unconventional behaviour."

"No, you condemn them for being too conventional," he said, somewhat smugly.

"You don't know what you're talking about. You've barely met her. When you know her as well as I do, then maybe I'll listen to what you have to say."

He put his arm around me.

"Truth hurts, I know," he said, kissing the top of my head, gently, in the condescending way that both infuriates and comforts me.

We lay in silence for a while.

"So, who else did you interview today?" I asked.

"Enough with the meddling," he murmured.

"I'm not meddling, I'm just taking an interest in the man's interests, like the teen magazines used to tell me."

"I've got other interests, too, you know," he said, sliding down next to me and reaching up under my tee-shirt.

After a few delicious minutes, I slipped out of bed.

"Where are you going?"

"I'll be right back."

I stumbled through the darkness to the dresser and fumbled around in the top drawer until I found the surprise I'd bought in the washroom in Davidson. Virna's home town. I unwrapped it and got back into bed, leaving my tee-shirt on the floor.

"It's a Nite-Glow," I whispered in his ear. "I want to watch the glow grow and grow."

So we did. We watched it glow, grow, crow, sing, dance, and practically whistle Dixie. Afterwards, we lay tangled together in the sheets.

"You still say I'm just like my mum?"

"You never know, Kate. She and your dad may have been wild in their time. They still might be."

"Are you kidding? They only did it twice. Once for Sheila and once for me."

"Then how do you explain your insatiable lust? Who did you inherit that from?"

"Maybe she had a passionate interlude with some passing stranger."

"Probably," Andy said. "With the bible salesman."

"Mr. Cyril Honeycutt. He was a pretty horny guy."

We both laughed in the darkness, feeling warm and close.

"So, you had drinks with Jack again tonight," Andy said, too casually.

"Edna and I, both. He's in pretty rough shape right now. We figured he could use some company."

"What have you been talking about?"

"His mother, mainly. Growing up with her and Wilma Elshaw. He's pretty devastated by their deaths."

"I guess he didn't happen to mention that he and his mother offed dear Auntie Wilma?"

I didn't answer for a moment.

"I guess your new best friend didn't happen to mention that," Andy said.

"Stop calling him that," I said. "Edna told me there had been some rumours. Did you talk to him about it?"

"He didn't deny it. He talked about the pain she was in at the end. How she died holding his mother's and his hands, with a smile on her face."

"And you call that murder?"

"What do you call it?"

"Mercy. Love. The kindest and most difficult thing any one can do. What I would hope you'd do for me if I asked. What I hope I'd have the courage to do for you."

The next silence was his. He held me very close.

"Who do your horsemen like as a suspect?" I asked, after a few minutes.

"At the moment, my horsemen are going off in all directions," he said. "Like the musical ride on acid. I think maybe the succession of old dears through the interview room was a bit too much for them. We're all going to sleep on it and start fresh in the morning."

He yawned.

"Well, I hope it goes better tomorrow, then," I said. "There are a lot of frightened people around here. Me included."

Our next silence lasted a long time. Almost into sleep. Then I remembered.

"Who do you like?" I asked him.

"For the murder?" he asked, sleepily.

"Uh huh."

"You know what they say. Who gains? I'm not quite ready to write off the next of kin."

CHAPTER

22

I called my editor, Jake Watson, first thing the next day and told him my plans for a feature on the girls' league. He told me to go ahead, as long as I hooked it on the murder. Then I called Dave Shury, the Hall of Fame guy, and arranged to have a look at the archives. After checking with the police, he told me to find the key, on a hook under the eaves at the back of the church. I promised to lock up when I was done. By ten-thirty, I was dug in with the All-American Girls Professional Baseball League files in the Hall of Fame library. Andy had dropped me off on the way to the RCMP, promising to pick me up in time for lunch.

There were signs of the investigation everywhere. I had to wipe grimy fingerprint powder off the desk and chair before I could use them. But I enjoy research, and quickly got so engrossed in the files that I almost forgot that I was sitting just a few feet away from where Virna Wilton had been found.

I skimmed a couple of turgid scholarly papers on the league, including one by the banquet speaker, and set aside a book that had been published a few years before, which Shury had said I could borrow. What interested me most that day was the primary material, the files and scrapbooks the women had brought with them to the reunion. They hadn't been catalogued or organized in any way yet. They just sat in cardboard boxes which had been brought over from the banquet hall.

I started with the old *Life* magazine piece from the first spring training in 1943. It was wonderfully politically incorrect, with photographs of Virna ironing in the locker room and Millie Epp of the Kenosha Comets having her hair done.

There was a lot of emphasis in the text on the wholesome aspects of the sport, on the charm school the girls attended, on the beauty makeovers by Helena Rubinstein, and on the credentials of the team chaperones. The other main thread of the piece was true-blue All-American patriotism, bringing entertainment to the home front while the boys were off fighting the war. One full-page photo showed the Racine Belles and Rockford Peaches, later arch-rivals, lined up along the basepaths in a "V for victory" formation, hats held over their hearts. My mother was way out at the far tip of one of the arms of the V.

After I finished that piece, I began to dig into the individual files and scrapbooks. I put aside the ones from the women on other teams and started by concentrating on the ones from the Saskatchewan Belles: Virna Wilton,

Edna Adams Summers, Shirley Rosen Goodman, Margaret Kostecki Deneka, Helen MacLaren Henry, and the late Wilma Elshaw.

Virna's was the fattest file, with articles from dozens of different papers. I could understand why she got the most ink: she was the lazy journalist's dream – good-looking, well-spoken, and, almost incidently, a terrific ballplayer. She also had what they then called great gams, which didn't hurt.

The other thing obvious from her carefully organized scrapbooks was that Virna never met a camera she didn't like, and knew how to give a good quote, even in those less media-savvy times. More power to her. She used what she had to get everything she could. She had a great career, and parleyed it into another one after the league folded. The later scrapbooks, after 1954, were almost as interesting as the ones when she was a star.

I looked closely at a picture of Virna and Wilma standing outside the All-American All-Star Flower Shoppe in 1956. Virna, who must have been in her middle thirties at the time, posed grinning, dressed in a dress that was the height of fifties fashion, with a bat on her shoulder. Wilma stood next to her, in slacks, her hair cropped short. She was smiling shyly, with her baseball and glove looking like props in her hands.

It was a feature article from the Women's Page of the Fort Wayne *News-Sentinel*, back when women's pages hadn't turned into the euphemistic Family or Lifestyle sections. Virna was portrayed as a plucky widow, raising her twelve-year-old son with the help of her old teammate Wilma. There was a picture of Jack with his dog, Morley. He was cute even then, a pre-adolescent hunk.

The post-career book apparently included every mention ever made of Virna, even references to the flowers for a ladies' tea or social being supplied by the shop. There were also speeches she'd made, community awards she had received, golf tournaments she had played in, and little-league teams she had coached.

By the time I'd put the last book aside, I knew more about Virna than I had before. I think I liked her less.

I skimmed my mother's scrapbook next. She wasn't a star, in talent or temperament, so there was less to read. Most of it I half-remembered from my childhood, anyway. Mum was a team player, there's that to be said about her. Any time she was quoted, it was to praise another player. And when other players talked about her, they applauded her unselfish nature. Having met my share of modern superstars and bench-warmers, I could read between the lines and understand how appreciated she was.

Generally, the young women I read about in the yellowed clippings were very like the older women I had come to know over the past few days. Rosie Rosen, as she then was, was garrulous and self-centred, slightly whiny and always ready with an excuse when she lost. She was also extremely glamorous in her playing days. She retired after the 1950 season. The last clipping in her scrapbook was the announcement of her marriage to "successful businessman Bert Goodman" and their subsequent round-the-world honeymoon cruise.

Edna Adams was then, as now, cute and likable, funny, energetic, and lacking in guile. She was obviously the team cheerleader and a fan favourite. Almost every story about her mentioned the championship home run.

When she retired, also in 1950, the community held an "Edna Adams Day" and gave her a set of matching luggage and a fur stole.

I was particularly intrigued by Margaret Deneka's file, because she was the one I could least imagine in her prime. As "Meg-the-Peg" Kostecki, she was one of the original Belles, a four-time all-star and, as Edna had implied, a real character. The term "live-wire" was used to describe her in several articles. She even made the gossip columns for pranks she pulled. I assumed they were her pranks. Why else would she have included in her scrapbook an item about ducks found swimming in the chaperone's hotel bathtub?

In her pictures, Meg was lovely, in an ethereal sort of way, almost angelic, with soft blonde hair framing a heart-shaped face, but mischief lurked in her eyes. In pictures of the Belles' keystone combination, she and Virna made a wonderful contrast: the one striking and dramatic, the other soft and feminine.

I turned to Wilma's material last. It was less orderly than Virna's, little more than a collection of clippings in annual file folders, covering only the years she played. I started with 1944, the year she and Edna joined the Belles. She made an immediate impression, hitting .319 in her rookie season. Sorting the clippings by date, I read a series of increasingly enthusiastic game stories, and a full personality profile towards the end of the season, angled towards women, and written by a woman who was clearly not in the sports department.

"Some say that baseball is a man's game," it began, "but Wilma Elshaw shows that a ballplayer can be a lady, too."

The saccharine story played up Wilma's domestic side, the needlework she did in her spare time and the warm mufflers she knit for the brave young men, including her fiancé, who were off at war, defending democracy.

"For Wilma Elshaw," the piece concluded, "all the cheers from all the fans in the baseball park are nice, but she dreams of accomplishments in another field. This Canadian All-American Girl looks forward to the day that a certain Royal Canadian Navy battleship comes in and she can embark on her next career as Mrs. Lieutenant Morley Timms."

That was an interesting development.

CHAPTER

23

When Andy went to the RCMP detachment that morning, the receptionist buzzed him through the inner door before he could state his business.

"Good morning, Inspector Munro. I hear that you're one of us," she said. "From the big city. The big, *big* city. Here to show us how?"

"I'm sure no one here needs any showing."

She got up from the desk and came around it with her hand extended in greeting. She was what is generously described as a "big-boned gal" in the prairies, with her red hair buzzed short. She wore open-toed sandals with her tailored slacks and shirt, and her toenails were painted an incongruous hot-pink.

"Anything I can do to help, let me know," she said, as they shook hands. "The name's Brenda Rasminsky, but everybody calls me Bambi."

Andy thanked her while trying to recall if he had ever encountered anyone less fawnlike in his life.

"The boys are waiting on you in the GIS office," she continued. "How do you take your coffee?"

"Three sugars, I'm afraid."

"Hey, you're a cop. It's not like sugar's the biggest risk you're ever going to take in your life. I'll bring the coffee on in. I'm just brewing a fresh pot."

"Thanks. Thanks, uh, Bambi. I appreciate it."

"After this, you fetch your own," she said.

"Always do."

"Glad to hear it," she said.

He went to the General Investigation Section, checking his watch on the way. They weren't due to start the meeting until ten, and he made it five minutes to.

Deutsch looked up when he rapped on the door jamb.

"Morning," he said, abruptly. "You can take the desk in the corner there for now. Then we can get this thing going."

Andy did as he was told, trying not to get annoyed by the chip on his colleague's shoulder. He sat at the desk and looked around the room at the rest of the assembled team, which consisted of Corporal Hugh Grenfell and constables Louis Tremblay and Dewey Resnick. A large work table had been cleared off for the investigation, with file folders and racks set up and ready to fill. A stack of index cards sat next to an empty metal box. Two laminated white boards leaned against the wall, their markers attached by strings.

A few minutes after Andy arrived, Inspector Digby and Staff Sergeant Morris came in and sat down.

"All right, gentleman," Digby said. "What have you got

for us? I've already got the press on my ass, local, national, and the U.S. I'd really like to get this one solved fast."

"You're not the only one," Deutsch said.

The meeting was pretty much like the ones Andy was used to in Toronto, except that there he was the one in charge. Deutsch started by going over the physical evidence at the scene and the pathologist's report.

"Death took place at the Hall, not elsewhere. It was, as we thought, caused by ligature strangulation, since there were no fingerprints or cuts on her throat. The killer used a piece of cloth of some sort, something soft, not a rope, not a wire. They picked up fibres from her neck. There were also contusions and bruising behind the ear, so we think she was knocked unconscious first. We've taken all the bats from the hall for fingerprinting, but I don't have much hope there. Too many people have touched them over the years."

"What about elsewhere in the Hall?"

"We got all sorts of prints from around the organ, but we have the same problem with those. It's a public place."

He flipped a few pages in the report.

"We've taken the seal off the Hall, by the way. Dave Shury called this morning to ask if that woman from Toronto could go in and do some research. Munro's friend."

"She's there now," Andy said. "Working on an article about the league."

"I hope that's all she's working on. You said yesterday that she has a habit of interfering with investigations."

"She has promised that if she comes up with anything that might have a bearing on the case she'll pass it along," Andy said, a bit defensively. "She's looking into the

153

history of the league and some of the women who were here. If this murder has its roots in the past, she might find them in those old files. If not, at least she's out of our hair."

Deutsch grunted and continued his report.

"There were no real surprises in the autopsy. Blood alcohol was high, .14, almost twice the legal limit, but we already knew that she'd had a few. Stomach contents confirm that her last meal was the one served at the banquet that night."

"Did it give him any reading on time of death?" Andy asked.

"I don't know what pathologists are like in your neck of the woods, but ours is super-cautious. Based on gastric testing and degree of rigor, he's given us a wide enough time margin to actually include the last time she was seen alive and when she was found."

"Thanks for nothing," Morris said.

"What about the other physical evidence?" Digby asked. "Any blood? Anything we can get DNA from?"

"The only blood was probably her own, from the head injury," Deutsch said. "Same blood type. No signs of struggle, no skin under the fingernails. We have some hairs, of different types. But they could be from any time."

"The public place problem again," Morris said.

"And a public place that isn't exactly a laboratory at the best of times," Grenfell added. "Old Morley Timms is the caretaker, and he just gives it a sweep or a mop when the mood takes him."

"Check when he cleaned it last," Deutsch said. Grenfell made a note.

"We did find one thing that might be significant. A button. Like from a suit jacket. With any luck, we can match it if we find a suspect."

"If, if, if," Digby said. "Any indication of the kind of strength required to strangle someone like this? Could it have been a woman? An old woman? Is that possible?"

"Pathologist thinks so. Especially since she was unconscious at the time. All someone would have to do is give her that bop on the head. After that she's not going to be resisting."

"But the murderer would have to lift her body onto the piano stool, there. That takes some strength."

"We can probably rule out the one with the walker," Deutsch said. "And that one who's all crippled up."

"That would be Edna Summers and Shirley Goodman," Andy said. "Then there's Mrs. Deneka, who is a few marbles short of a bag."

"Come on, I can't see one of those old biddies doing it," Resnick said, impatiently.

"They can't be ruled out if the motive is in the past," Andy pointed out.

"That's a big if," Resnick said. Tremblay shot a look at Andy to see how he'd react to this insubordination. He didn't.

"Let's get back to work," Deutsch said. "You all did good work yesterday, which may or may not turn out to be relevant. Now we expand the investigation. Tremblay, Resnick, you'll concentrate on finding as many of the people who were in the bar Saturday night as you can. You can use some of the uniforms for legwork. I want them all tracked down. Start with the bartender. He'll know who the regulars were. Hugh, you go back to the hotel and talk

155

to any hotel guest who was there that night, whether or not they are connected with the Hall of Fame thing. Someone might have seen or heard something. Door to door. Get back to me as soon as you can. Any questions?"

No one volunteered. They got to their feet, not looking happy about the drudgery that faced them, and headed out the door.

"What do you want me to do?" Andy asked.

"You and I are going to go through those interviews from yesterday and look for that motive from the past. If that's all right with you."

"I agree that's a good place to look," Andy said, unsure if he had read sarcasm in Deutsch's voice. "Just because one of her team-mates didn't do it, it doesn't mean they weren't involved."

"Or they know something they're not telling. Let's get another coffee and get started. Where do you want to start?"

"With the son. Jack Wilton."

"You like him?"

"Closest to the victim," Andy said. "As good a place to begin as any."

"Tell you what. I'll go through one stack, you go through another, then we'll switch and talk about it."

"You mentioned coffee," Andy said.

"I'll show you where the pot's kept. Come with me."

Andy followed him down the hall to the lunchroom, which was empty. They filled two cups, added sugar, and went back up the hall.

They spent the next hour reading files, doing the boring routine work out of which blinding insights sometimes come.

CHAPTER

24

Andy picked me up at one o'clock with the news that he couldn't have lunch with me, but he drove me back to the hotel. He went to the room to pick up his address book, and I went looking for my parents. I knew they had planned to meet Edna by the pool for lunch and I found them all there. I told them about my morning's researches.

"Did you know that Wilma Elshaw once planned to marry Morley Timms?"

"That peculiar round fellow?" my father asked. "She was engaged to him?"

"According to an article in her files, yes."

"I'm not sure I knew about that," my mother said. "If I did, I'd forgotten."

"Did her relationship with Virna get in the way?" I pressed. This was no time for my mother's delicacy. "Did she break it off with him because she became a lesbian?"

"Dear, we don't know that, do we? She and Virna might have been just good friends."

"Mum, I've seen the photos. Once she got out from under the charm school rules of the league, she was butch city."

"There's no need to be vulgar."

"I'm sorry, but this could be significant. He could have been holding a grudge against Virna all these years."

"But that fellow is obviously harmless," my father said.

"But this gives him the motive, don't you see? Who could I ask about this who would know why the wedding got called off? Maybe I'll ask Garth Elshaw. He would know."

"Do you think you should be asking him things like that about his own sister?" my mother asked.

"Well, someone in town must know."

"Why don't you leave it to Andy and the other officers," my father said.

"Leave what to Andy?" he asked, appearing as if by magic next to the table.

"Hello, Andy, pull up a chair," Edna said. "Kate's tracked down a hot clue."

"Why am I not surprised?" he asked. "Thanks, but I can't stay. What do you think you've got now, Kate?"

I explained about Morley Timms and Wilma Elshaw.

"No, we didn't know that," he said. "At least I didn't. I'll pass the word along."

He checked his watch.

"I've got to go. I'll see you later."

"How's the investigation going?" Edna asked.

"Just plugging along," he said.

158

"No convenient dramatic confessions like they get on television?" I asked.

"No such luck, just a bunch of bored cops going door to door and shuffling paper."

"Aren't you staying for lunch?" Edna asked.

"There's a sandwich waiting at the office," he said. "If you want the car, Kate, you can drive me back there."

"No, I've got material to work with here. That's all right. That place gives me the creeps, anyway."

"If you need a car, you can borrow ours, Kate," my father said, then addressed Andy. "Will you be having supper with us?"

"I might not be through in time. I'll have to let you know."

"Before six, mind you," my mother said.

"Of course," Andy smiled.

"And if you're not ready, I can wait for you," I said.

"Oh, no, I wouldn't want to keep you waiting for your food. I might not be finished until after seven."

I was the only one who saw his wink.

After lunch, feeling too restless to work on my article, I did borrow my parents' car and drove into Battleford. It was a hot, dry day, with wind swirling the dust in the parking lot next to the Fred Light museum. I parked and wandered to the back of the lot to look down at the North Saskatchewan River curving in the valley below. It was pretty. I could see a baseball game in progress on a diamond in the riverside park, too far away for me to follow it, but I stood awhile and watched the familiar patterns. It was soothing.

A small brown puppy, which had been doing some fearless hunting in the underbrush, ran over to investigate the stranger, decided he liked her, and jumped up to offer friendship. I took a stick and threw it for him to fetch. It was a game he clearly knew, and one I tired of before he did. I decided to tour the museum, for lack of anything more interesting to do. The puppy followed me hopefully to the door, stick in mouth. I threw it for him one more time, then feeling vaguely guilty, slipped into the museum and shut the door behind me.

I don't know why Saskatchewan has so many local museums, but there's hardly a town that doesn't have some sort of repository of its history. I've been to a few of them over the years, and they have a reassuring similarity. The Fred Light, evidently named for the man whose collection began the museum, followed the same sort of pattern. There was a room done up like an old general store, with long-forgotten products and laughably low prices on the shelves. Then there was a kitchen and a parlour with their displays of household items; an old doctor's office with scary-looking implements; a railway station waiting-room, with a mannequin dressed as a conductor. I wandered through the military history gallery, with uniforms from both world wars as well as from the old fort, and the adjacent room celebrating the area's native history, reflecting on the irony of the juxtaposition of those two cultures of mutual distrust.

I was the only visitor, and the silence was welcome and contemplative. While I peered into cases, I let my mind wander over the events of the past few days, and the people I had met.

Edna was my favourite. Her enthusiasm, energy, and humour were all so contagious that even my mother lightened up around her. Shirley Goodman, on the other hand, was a self-centred old bore who deserved being married to that fat little creep of a husband. Meg Deneka's combination of sweetness and bawdiness was startlingly wonderful, and I was half in love with her devoted big guy. It would have been nice to have known her before she began "talking to the birdies," as Edna had put it.

And, of course, Virna. Virna of the practical jokes; Virna with the nerve to show up at the banquet in her old uniform; Virna, the biggest star the All-American Girls Professional Baseball League ever had; Virna, the generous-spirited woman who gave such a gracious speech at the banquet; Virna, life of the party in the bar; Virna, the mother who inspired such devotion in her son; but also Virna of the scrapbooks, egocentric, self-serving, and vain; and finally, Virna the "unnatural" woman whose remains now lay in the indignity of the forensic laboratory in Regina. Why? Find the why and you've got the who. That's what Andy always says.

I was just heading out of the museum, when I was hailed by the volunteer at the museum's desk.

"Have you signed the guest book?"

I went to the desk and reached for the pen.

"I have to get everyone to sign in so we get our grant every year," she said. She was a large, red-faced woman in a sleeveless dress, with the broad, placid face of a peasant from a Brueghel painting, except for her tight curls of an improbable strawberry-blonde. Her name badge identified her as Gladys Bieber.

"We have to prove we had the visitors," she went on, rather breathlessly. I didn't dare disobey. After I'd signed, she turned it around.

"Toronto, eh? What brings you to Battleford?"

I explained about the Hall of Fame induction, which perked her right up.

"Oh, where that woman got murdered," she said, gleefully. "That's a terrible thing. Just terrible."

She looked at me, expectantly.

"Yes, it was terrible," I said, trying to edge towards the door.

"Did you know the dead woman?"

Curiosity gleamed from her little blue eyes.

"I had just met her the day of the banquet, but my mother knew her. They used to play on the same team."

"Did she, now? For the Racine Belles? Then she must have played with Wilma Elshaw, too."

"Yes, she did. Did you know Wilma?"

"I went all the way through school with Wilma Elshaw. We were best friends."

I let go of the door handle.

"Were you, now?" I asked.

CHAPTER

25

It didn't take much to get Gladys Bieber to offer me a cup of tea. There was a kettle and a small fridge on a table in a room just off the main hall.

Gladys explained that she had retired ten years before, but until then had been the history teacher at the high school. No, she'd never married, but all her students were like family to her. She told me of the accomplishments of some of her favourites while we waited for the kettle to boil. The mayor had been a prize pupil, as had the Member of Parliament for The Battlefords–Meadow Lake and the current high school principal.

"I like to think I instilled the love of education in him, and a sense of history in the other two," she said. "Now maybe one of them can become a part of history."

Any doubts I had about the history-making potential of a small-town mayor or a backbencher in the House of Commons were ones I kept to myself. Gladys paused long enough to open a cupboard where she kept, no surprise, a stash of cookies.

"Tell me about Wilma," I said. "I wish I'd had a chance to meet her. She seems so interesting from what I've heard or read."

"Oh, she was. She was interesting and nice as pie. You should have known her then."

"Was she kind of a tomboy when you were growing up? With the baseball-playing and all."

"Not a bit of it. No, she was never a tomboy."

Gladys kind of glared at me, and I realized that I must have inadvertently stumbled on a code word to make her so indignant.

"She was just the opposite, in fact. She was all girl. She just happened to love baseball. I did too. Of course I wasn't ever as good as she was, but when we were young, we all played. We played on the church team."

As if that settled that.

"Oh, I know what everybody said. I wasn't born yesterday, you know. But as I sit here telling you, Wilma Elshaw was all girl. Normal, I mean."

"There was a lot of gossip those days, wasn't there? I know my mother had problems with some people in Wolseley where she came from. They didn't think women should play baseball."

"Just goes to show what they know, doesn't it. N-o-t-h-i-n-g spells nothing. That's what they know."

"I was just reading some files at the Hall of Fame. There was an article about her knitting scarves for the boys at the front."

"You see, that was just like Wilma, always thinking of others. She had a lovely hand at needlepoint, too."

164

"So the article said."

"I still have the knitting bag she made for me the first year she played in the league. I still have it, more than fifty years later. It's lovely work."

"The article said she was engaged," I tried.

Gladys looked a little uncomfortable.

"What happened?"

"Well, that was a bit of a mystery, you know," she almost whispered, looking around as if for eavesdroppers or hidden microphones. "I grew up with Morley Timms, too. That was her fiancé."

"Yes, I've met him," I said.

"Well, you haven't met the Morley Timms that went off to war. You've met the one who came back."

"You mean something happened to him? He was injured?"

"The Morley that went off to war with Garth Elshaw was a real catch. All the girls were in love with him back then. You should have seen him. He was so gay!"

She took another cookie.

"And I don't mean gay the way they use it today. They took a perfectly good word and made it dirty. But there's no other word to describe Morley as he was back then. Happy-go-lucky, merry. He always had a smile on his face and a joke on his lips. He was a wonderful singer, and he loved to dance. Oh, and he was smart, too. No two ways about it. His future was bright."

"And he and Wilma were going to share that future," I said.

"They'd known it since they were kids. They all grew up together. Garth and Morley were best friends then."

"As they are now."

"Well, now it's more that Garth looks out for him. Then, Morley was the one. Garth just sort of tagged along in his shadow. But they were a formidable pair. At first, Wilma was just the kid sister, but that changed as she got older. She got such a crush on Morley. I had a crush on Garth, too. But the day Morley realized that Wilma had grown up, that was that. Unfortunately, Garth never came to that conclusion about me."

She laughed, not bitterly, and grabbed another cookie.

"He played the field, Garth did. He didn't marry until he was in his thirties. We thought he was going to be a bachelor for life, but he surprised us all. Married a widow with two sons, so he had himself a ready-made family."

I didn't know how to get her back to Morley and Wilma without obviously interrogating her, so just waited her out.

"Yes, he broke some hearts. A lot of people in this town, not just me, thought that if he married anyone, it was going to be me. We kept company for a while after the war, but I just never lit his fire, I guess."

"He changed after the war, then."

"Oh, yes. He was more serious, kind of withdrawn. He'd lost his sense of fun. He never talked about what he'd seen there, but Garth's sense of adventure was gone when he came back."

"Maybe because war is the most deadly adventure."

"Morley, now, he came home a different man altogether. He hasn't been quite right ever since. It's a real shame."

She took another cookie to fuel the narrative.

"They had to put him in the mental hospital for a while, even. He was wild. One day he'd be laughing and joking just like the old days. The next he wouldn't hardly

166

say a word. He took to drinking. Not that he hadn't had a nip or two from the flask before. I mean, who didn't? But this was different. And he'd get out there in his car and drive like a maniac. I remember one night after a dance over to Maidstone he almost scared us all to death. He was driving the gang back in a snowstorm. We were all singing and laughing, we'd had a few, when Morley suddenly says he's going to make the car fly. We all laugh, but Morley says he can do it, and then just begins going faster and faster and faster, and swearing at the car and telling us to stick our arms out the window, I remember it like it was yesterday."

Clearly, she did. Poor Gladys had become increasingly agitated, telling the story. Her cheeks had turned quite pink.

"We all thought we were going to die, truly," she said. "I never rode with him again, I'll tell you that. If it hadn't been for Garth, I don't know what would have happened that night."

"What did Garth do?"

"He just talked to him, talked him down, like. Wilma and I were screaming and crying and begging him to stop. Garth just leaned forward over the seat, he was in the back with me, and talked to him real quiet, in his ear. And Morley just let his foot off the pedal a little bit, then a little bit more, and then just stopped the car, right in the middle of the highway. And then he began to cry and cry. I've never seen a man cry like that before. He cried like a little kid, just blubbering. Then we all got out of the car, and Garth got him to move over and let him drive. And Morley cried all the rest of the way home. Next day they took him right to the Saskatchewan

Hospital, they called it the asylum then, and he was in there for a long time."

"So Wilma was there that night?"

"Yes, she was. She was right next to him. All the way home, she held him in her arms and he cried like he was her baby."

"So she called the wedding off?"

"No, it wasn't her. It was him. She was prepared to stick by him through thick and thin, Wilma was. She went to see him every day at the hospital, and he just refused to talk to her. He just sat staring at the wall, she told me. She didn't know what to do. So when spring rolled around, she just decided to go back to baseball, and she never came home again, except to visit."

"That's very sad," I said.

"And once she hooked up with that Virna, she changed."

"How?"

"She just kind of hardened her heart. After Morley got better, maybe he wanted to marry her. But it was too late. And I can't say as I blame her. Because Morley still acted pretty cuckoo, if you want to know the truth. He never did hold down a real job, and he became kind of the town eccentric, wandering around at all hours, dressed in all manner of strange get-ups. But likable, you know? He wasn't dangerous or anything. They gave him some kind of shock therapy, like they did in those days, and some sort of experimental surgery, and he just sort of flattened out. He lost part of his mind, I guess. He was never as wild again, but he didn't have any drive and he wasn't smart any more. Well, you've met him. That's how he's been ever since."

The front door opened, and we heard the clatter of footsteps and the chatter of voices. Gladys looked at her watch.

"Oh, my goodness, I've been babbling on and not looking at the time. Here's my group from the Golden Years Lodge. I'm afraid I'm going to have my hands full for a while."

She got heavily to her feet and went to the door. I followed her, thanking her for the tea and her kindness to a stranger.

"You know what I always say, dear," she said, patting my arm. "A stranger's just a friend you haven't met yet."

CHAPTER

26

By four that afternoon, Andy and Deutsch had finished reading through the interview transcripts and statements from all of the people who had been at the banquet. Grenfell, Tremblay, and Resnick came back to report on their first round of door-to-door.

"What've you got?" Deutsch asked. "Start with you, Tremblay. Who was at the bar?"

"First we had to find the bartender, Rock. He wasn't at home."

"He was shacked up with his squeeze," Resnick laughed. "He wasn't pleased to see us. He was so hungover he didn't know which way was up."

"I don't care about the state of his health," Deutsch said. "What did he tell you?"

"He gave us a list of the people he remembered, about twenty of them," Tremblay said. "Some names already known to this office."

"A bunch of rounders, for sure," Resnick added.

"We talked to as many as we could find, and got more names from them. We're up to fifty-three, now, in addition to the ones we knew about already. The constables are still out talking to them, but we ran the names through the computer. And we've come up with something interesting."

"Yeah, wait 'til you hear this, Sarge," Resnick added. "We've got a live one."

"Nathan Rowley," Tremblay interrupted, glaring. "He's got a record that you should know about."

"Never heard of him," Deutsch said.

"He's new in town. He lives with his aunt, Ruth Fernie, over on 28th Street near the Convention Centre."

"Ruth Fernie? The Ruth Fernie from the Hall of Fame?" Andy asked. "She found the body."

"Exactly. The same Ruth Fernie. Rowley is her nephew. He's been staying with her for the last four months, working in the Wal-Mart warehouse."

"You going to get around to telling me what's interesting about this guy any time soon?" Deutsch asked.

"He's on parole. He served three years for a series of assaults in Saskatoon," Tremblay said.

"Yeah? So what?"

"He specialized in old ladies, Sarge," Resnick said. "That's so what. Broke into their houses in broad daylight, roughed them up and stole their money. But it seemed like he enjoyed the rough stuff. They never had much cash, and he didn't take anything else. TVs or anything like that he could sell."

"Have you got a printout?" Deutsch asked.

"Right here, sir," Tremblay said, handing it to him.

"Good work," Deutsch said, then began to read. Tremblay shot his partner a smug glance, pleased with the boss's approval.

"I'm going to call the arresting officer in Saskatoon on this," Deutsch said. "See if he can tell me any more about this character."

He went to a phone at the other end of the office.

"You guys go on," he added. "Tell Andy what else you've turned up."

"Has anyone talked to Rowley yet?" Andy asked.

"No, we just learned about his record," Tremblay said.

"You said some of the others in the bar are known to the police."

"Nobody as interesting as him," Resnick said. "Got guys did some B and Es, drunk driving, cigarette smuggling. A couple of hookers in there, and their pimps. Small stuff. One guy can't stop beating on his wife. But nobody looks as good as Rowley. Just feels right."

Deutsch came back from the phone.

"The guy who handled the case down there says that none of the women were killed, but he threatened them with it. Terrorized them, played with them, made sure they got really scared. One of them he choked until she was unconscious, but she lived. Another thing. He didn't steal the big stuff, but he always took something away from the scene. A small piece of jewellery, a porcelain figurine."

"A trophy," Andy interrupted.

"Exactly."

"It would be nice to get a look at his house. Can we get a warrant?"

"I don't think we've got enough to convince a judge

yet," Deutsch said. "But I think we'll invite Mr. Rowley in for a little chat this afternoon. Hugh, find out when he gets off work. Have someone waiting for him when he gets home."

"Why not do a follow-up on Ruth Fernie's statement?" Andy suggested.

"Good idea," Deutsch said. "It's a legitimate reason to be there, and maybe have a little look-see at the situation. Go for it, Hugh. But first, give us what you picked up at the hotel."

Corporal Grenfell flipped open his notebook.

"A number of people heard a commotion in the back parking lot after about one in the morning, when the bar let out. Yelling, a woman screamed, but when they looked out the window, there were a bunch of people around, and it didn't look like anyone was in trouble. A little later, Reverend Henry got up to go to the bathroom, he thinks it was just after two, and he heard a truck pull out of the parking lot. He couldn't see who was in it, but he's pretty sure he heard two doors close."

He looked up from the notes.

"Then Peter Deneka was up at about 5:30. He says even a retired farmer always wakes up early. Anyway, he saw another pickup truck pulling out, and wondered if someone was skipping out on the bill."

"Christ, from what I've seen around here, everybody drives pickup trucks," Andy said. "That's not much of a clue."

"You're right," Deutsch said. "I drive one myself."

"That's all. I've got home addresses on some people who checked out," Grenfell said. "You want me to follow them up now, or go get Rowley?"

"Go to the Fernie house. Leave your notes here. Dewey, I want you to put together a time chart we can plug the information into as it comes in. Try to get a handle on who was where, when."

"What about me?" Tremblay asked.

"You get the information from the other guys as they come in and put it in some sort of form for your buddy to use."

Andy could see that neither was pleased with his assignment. But that's the way it worked in every police force. The constable is trusted to dig up the lead, but not to follow it through.

"I've been thinking," Andy said. "Maybe we can't charge him with anything yet, but I bet we could bring him in for parole violation. I bet there's a clause in there that says he has to stay away from liquor and bad company."

"Bingo," Deutsch said. "We've got to have that information somewhere around here. Louis. See what you can get. Look in the computer. If you have to call the parole office in Saskatoon, do it."

"Right away, Sergeant."

"Faster than that, if you can," Deutsch said.

CHAPTER

27

I spent the next couple of hours reading the research material that I'd borrowed from the Hall and putting my notes from that morning in order. Then I lay down with a book, which ended up face-down on my chest. When I stopped contemplating the insides of my eyelids, it was half-past five. I decided to call home to let them know Andy and I would be a few days late getting back.

We live in a three-storey brick house in the Riverdale neighbourhood of Toronto. I bought it with a former lover back in the days when anything east of the Don River valley, which bisects the city, was considered so declassé that even a normal working stiff could afford a house there. Now, the area is positively trendy, and my house is worth more than my parents' whole block in Indian Head, which shows how crazy things are in this country. I could sell my fairly modest place and buy a mansion anywhere else in Canada.

About ten years ago, when the relationship broke up, I bought out his share and turned the house into a duplex so I could afford the mortgage. Andy and I have the top two floors and I rent out the first floor and basement to my friend Sally Parkes and her son, T.C., who has grown into a teenager under my roof. He answered the phone in the deep voice I'm still not used to.

"Hey, T.C., how are you?"

"Hey, Kate. Where are you?"

I explained.

"Cool," he said. "Another body drops at your feet. Have you ever thought about maybe hiring yourself out as some sort of karmic hit man? Hit woman."

"Very funny."

"No, listen. Say someone wants to get back at some enemy, right? So you get a fee up front to just, like, go visit the guy, and it's easily fifty-fifty something bad's going to happen to him. If it does, you get the rest. I'll be your agent. We'll get rich."

"T.C., put a lid on that imagination. You've been reading too much science fiction. Is your mum around?"

"No, she and Tip are at the vet."

Tip Keenan, a private detective who had once been a colleague of Andy's, had been involved in finding a missing woman in our neighbourhood the previous year, and had been involved with Sally since then. He's a nice guy, and has made a great and pleasant difference in all our lives.

"Why? Is something wrong with Martha?"

Martha is T.C.'s foster dog, a sweet mutt who came into our lives at the same time as Tip.

"No, it's Elwy, he's just being a bit weird."

My heart sank. My cat, Elwy, is pushing twenty. Lately he has been showing some creakiness in his joints and crankiness in his disposition, but he's been otherwise fine.

"Weird, how?" I asked.

"Well, he's not eating, for one thing."

"That's hardly going to hurt him," I said, trying to laugh.

"Right. And he was meowing a lot. But it's been really hot, so that might be what's wrong. Anyway, Mum took him in just to make sure everything's okay."

"Thank her for me. And tell her to phone me when she gets back. Use my phone so it won't go on your bill."

I gave him the number and hung up. When Andy called a few minutes later, I almost burst into tears when I told him.

"That's too bad. But he's had a lot of good years."

Andy tolerates cats, but just doesn't get my bond with Elwy.

"He's not dead yet," I said, angrily. "He's probably fine. I just feel badly that I'm not there with him when he's . . ."

I choked up again.

"Are you all right, Kate?"

"No, I'm not all right. But thanks for asking."

"Kate, what are you getting yourself so worked up about? He's only a cat. And you've been expecting him to die ever since I've known you."

"That doesn't make it any better."

"I'm sorry. I'm sorry you're upset. I hope you hear some good news soon. We'll talk about it when I get back."

"When will that be?"

"It might be an hour, it might be two. There have been some developments."

"What kind of developments?"

"I can't talk about it right now. Anyway, maybe you'd better have dinner with your parents."

"I can't face the early-bird special. I'll wait for you. I mean, you have to eat sometime, right?"

"Okay, I'll give you a call before seven to let you know."

"I'll be here, or in the bar, if I find some company. Edna would probably like someone to have her cocktail with."

"Or your new best friend Jack," he said.

"Your favourite suspect, you mean?"

"He's getting less favourite every minute," Andy said.

"Why?"

"I can't tell you right now."

"So you're happy for me to go drinking with him?"

"I wouldn't go that far," he grumbled. "But you're a big girl, you can do what you want."

"You've got that right," I said. He grunted.

"Got to go. I hope Elwy's all right, really."

I called my parents next, to tell them I had to wait for a phone call from Toronto and they should go ahead without me.

"If you're sure," my father said. "I wouldn't mind waiting, except we have plans to meet with the Denekas and Edna."

"No, I need to know how Elwy is," I said.

"I understand," he said. "I feel the same way about Shadrach. Keep your chin up, and let me know what happens."

I managed to say goodbye without losing it completely, then sat on the bed feeling like an idiot. Why was I so upset? Andy is right. I've assumed that every winter would be Elwy's last since he was fifteen. And he *is* only a cat. A homely, portly, not very smart, old black-and-white alley cat.

I turned the television to the Titan game, which, with the time difference, was already underway, then curled up in the armchair and tried to let it divert me.

There's a strong bond between human and pet. Maybe because it is without words. Or maybe because it's the one love we give unconditionally, without keeping any of it held back because of fear of being hurt or betrayed.

We've been through a lot together, old Elwy and I. When he was a kitten, I was still in my twenties, living on my own and just starting to make it freelance, flying high and invincible. Anything was possible when Elwy and I started out.

It's amateur psychology time, ladies and gents. Elwy was, of course, my last link to that young and confident Kate Henry I'd mislaid somewhere along the way. My last link to that knock-'em-dead redhead who got lost somewhere under the wrinkles. Man, what a lot of emotional weight to give to seventeen pounds of fur and purr.

The phone rang. Sally, back from the vet.

"They're keeping him in overnight. He's dehydrated. I guess he hasn't been drinking enough water in all this heat. I'm sorry, Kate, I didn't notice anything was wrong until today."

"Sally. No reason to. Did they say what might be wrong?"

"The vet's going to run some tests. She says she wants to avoid exploratory surgery because of his age."

"What kind of tests?"

"Blood tests for liver and kidney function, like that. When a cat's as old as Elwy, any number of things can go wrong."

"Whatever it turns out to be, I don't want him to suffer."

"I know that. It probably won't come to that. Don't worry."

"Thanks for taking charge. I know it's not any fun for you, either."

"It's nothing, Kate. We love Elwy too."

Now she was getting weepy.

"This is silly," I said.

"No one has ever accused us of being sensible, my friend."

"Thank goodness for small blessings. Give my love to Tip."

"And ours to Andy. I'll talk to you tomorrow when I know something. And you let us know when you'll be coming back. We miss you."

"Me too."

I hung up and hugged myself in my chair, wishing Elwy was there to comfort me.

CHAPTER

28

Hugh Grenfell brought Nathan Rowley in just after six. He was a heavy man in his late twenties, dressed in jeans and a washed-out green Saskatchewan Roughriders tee-shirt. His dark blond hair was cut short in front and curled below the collar in back. His weedy moustache and goatee didn't do much for his looks, which could have used some help. His blue eyes were small and close-set, and his cheeks pitted with acne scars.

It doesn't matter, Andy thought, big city or small town, this is the kind of petty crook you can spot at a thousand paces.

"Mr. Rowley, thanks for coming in," Deutsch said, getting to his feet, smiling. He put out his hand. Rowley shook it warily.

Okay, Andy thought, as Deutsch introduced him to the suspect, now we know who's going to be good cop.

What's my role? He decided to settle for silent cop for the time being and see what was needed.

Rowley took the proffered chair and crossed his right ankle to his left knee. He betrayed his nervousness by jiggling his right foot, but otherwise seemed calm.

"Why we've invited you here, Mr. Rowley, is to ask you some questions about Saturday night," Deutsch said. "I guess you know that one of those older women that were at Shooters that night was murdered."

"I heard that, yeah," Rowley said.

"Well, now, I understand that you were there that night," Deutsch said, pleasantly, "and we were all hoping you could tell us what you remember. Did you see the women?"

"Sure," he said, helpfulness written all over his face. His toe tempo went up a notch. "I seen them. It was hard to miss. They're not the kind you usually see there on a Saturday night. Hall of Fame, eh? I saw it on TV."

"That's right," Deutsch said. "There was one of them in particular. You would have remembered her. She was wearing that yellow dress. The old-fashioned uniform with the skirt."

"I remember her. Jeez, was she the one that got killed?"

"Why is it you remember her?"

"Well, the uniform and all. That was pretty unusual. Me and my buddies from work, that's who I was with, some buddies from work, we were like, right at the next table, eh?"

"Go on," Deutsch said.

"Well, like we talked to her. We're on a softball team together, right? Me and my buddies from work. She said that she and the other old ladies could whip our butts. That's what she said. 'We could whip your butts. What do you think about that?' It was pretty comical."

"Yeah, comical," Deutsch said, mildly. "Did you happen to notice anything when they left, whether anyone followed them."

Rowley closed his eyes, the better to concentrate, no doubt, or the better to formulate a story. Then he shook his head.

"No, I didn't notice anything because we left before they did. Yeah, I remember now, they was all still sitting there when we left."

"You're sure of that?"

"Yeah, I'm sure," he said, nodding like one of those toy dogs in the back of a car. "Because we said goodbye to them when we left, because we'd been talking to them and all."

"What time was that, Nathan? Just to keep our records straight."

"Oh, like twelve-thirty. Not real late. Like I had to drop my buddies off first, and it wasn't one o'clock when I got home. My aunt, who I live with? She likes me to be home before one."

"I'm sure your aunt can back you up on this, Nathan? The time you got home."

"I don't know. She was in bed. Maybe she heard me. Why?"

"We're just trying to get the times straight, who left when, just to narrow things down."

"Well, it was definitely before one. I know that."

"And it took you half an hour to get home."

"Well, like I said, I had to drop my buddies off, eh? Maybe it was after twelve-thirty when we left, but not much after."

"And you spoke to the women before you left."

"Yeah, they were teasing us about whipping our butts, like I said. So we sort of teased them back. Told them to meet us at the ball diamond the next day. Just kidding around."

"How did they seem?"

"Oh, they was happy. They was a bit drunk if you want to know the truth. Kind of funny to see a bunch of old grannies shit-faced."

"You've got a thing about old grannies, right, Rowley?" Grenfell asked, quietly. Rowley's toe stopped tapping. Then Andy knew who bad cop was going to be.

"I don't know what you mean by that," Rowley said, avoiding Grenfell's gaze.

"Your record, Nathan," he said. "You don't think we know about that?"

"Wait a minute," Rowley said, looking from Grenfell to Deutsch, then to the other men in the room. When he got to Munro, silent cop just folded his arms and stared, as if at a zoo exhibit. "What's this about? You're trying to pin this on me because I've got a record? No way! You got the wrong guy."

"Calm down, Mr. Rowley. We're not charging you with anything. Corporal Grenfell, you shouldn't have frightened Mr. Rowley. He's just trying to help. He's cooperating. He's being a good citizen."

"Yeah, that's what I'm trying to do."

Grenfell sat back in his chair. Chastised.

"I'm sorry, sir," he said, eyes down.

"It's young Mr. Rowley you should be apologizing to, not me," Deutsch said.

Grenfell muttered something no one could hear. It might have been an apology.

"By the way, would you like a coffee or anything?" Deutsch asked. Rowley jumped at it.

"Hugh, get our guest a coffee," Deutsch said. Grenfell got to his feet and went out the door. On his way, with his back to the suspect, he winked at Andy, who had to cough behind his fist to hide his smile.

"You're doing fine, Mr. Rowley," Deutsch said. "Nothing to worry about."

"Listen, I just want to help," he said. "I did my time, and I'm rehabilitated. I've changed. That stuff before, I was drinking and doing a lot of drugs. Now I'm straight. I've got a job here, and a place to live, you know? I don't want to cause anybody any trouble, okay?"

"We don't want to cause you any trouble, either," Deutsch said. "Now, can you tell me the names of the buddies you were with. Names and addresses. Just to make sure we've got all the witnesses in place."

"Sure. Ernie McLeod, he lives here in North Battleford. Jimmy Kelly lives with his girlfriend over here, too. I drove them first. And Banjo Rasmussen, he's over near my aunt's place."

Deutsch pulled a list out from a file on his desk.

"Banjo Rasmussen. Would that be Benjamin Rasmussen? Is that his real name?"

"I guess so," Rowley shrugged. "Banjo's all I know."

"Well, good," Deutsch said. "We've got these names and numbers already. Just sit tight for a second. I'm going to make a few phone calls."

He went out the door, leaving Rowley alone with Andy. After a few minutes on silence, Rowley looked at Andy.

"How's it going?" he asked. No reply. "You don't talk a lot, do ya?" Nothing.

"Jeez," Rowley said. "I can't believe this. I hope you guys don't think I had anything to do with this."

He stood up and began to pace.

"Man, oh, man. I can't believe this."

Grenfell came back into the room and handed Rowley a Styrofoam cup. He took a sip and grimaced.

"Don't you got any sugar?"

"We're fresh out," Grenfell said, then turned to Andy.

"The punk said anything incriminating yet?"

"Hey, I don't have to listen to this shit," Rowley said. "You got no reason to call me names."

He slumped back down in his chair, his knees spread wide.

"Shut up, punk," Grenfell said, emphasizing the last word coldly. "We got you for breaking parole, at the very least."

"No way," Rowley said. "What are you talking about?"

"Your parole prohibits the use of alcohol or consorting with known felons."

"I wasn't drinking anything. Just Cokes. I was the designated driver. How much more law-abiding do you want me to be? I was doing you all a favour, keeping drunks off the road. And my buddies aren't what you call them, felons. They're just guys I work with at Wal-Mart. They don't have no records. You can look it up."

186

"No, they don't, punk, but I can name you seven other guys in that bar who do."

"But I wasn't with them."

"I don't think that technicality will get in our way if we decide we want to hold you, Mr. Law-and-Order," Grenfell said, sarcastically.

He sat glaring at Rowley, who didn't enjoy the attention. After a few moments of silence, Grenfell leaned forward so his face was just inches from Rowley's.

"What did you do, Nathan, wait for her outside the bar and jump her? Or did you follow her to her room?"

"I didn't do it. You've got to believe me, man."

"You're going down on this, Nathan. Make it easy on yourself. Tell us what happened."

"I want my lawyer," Rowley said.

"I bet you do," Grenfell said. "I just bet you do."

He sat back in his chair when Deutsch came back into the room. Rowley stood up.

"I don't have anything more to say," he said.

"Oh, let me be the judge of that," Deutsch said.

"I think Mr. Rowley is trying to tell you thinks he needs a lawyer," Andy said.

"I know my rights," Rowley said. "You have to let me talk to my lawyer."

"Relax, Nathan," Deutsch said. "We haven't charged you with anything. We are simply looking for information about that night. You have been cooperative so far, and we appreciate it."

Rowley glared at Hugh Grenfell.

"Tell him to back off, then," he said.

"Corporal, you're out of line," Deutsch said. "Now, we just have a few more loose ends to tie up. Thinking back on that night, did you see anyone else talk to the women at that table?"

"No. No one I knew, anyways. There were a couple of old guys in suits who said hello. And one old fat guy who was trying to get his wife to leave. She wouldn't though. That's all I saw."

"All right. That's very helpful. Now, I was just wondering something else. About the Hall of Fame. You've been there, I guess."

"Sure. I help out my aunt there sometimes when she's in charge."

"It's an interesting place. Lots of interesting things. You play ball yourself?"

"A bit. Just softball now. But I was a pretty good hitter in high school."

Deutsch nodded a few times, then rather abruptly stood up. He smiled and held out his hand.

"We won't need to trouble you any more today."

Rowley looked relieved.

"By the way," he added, as an afterthought, "who did you say your lawyer is?"

"Alan Cramdon," Rowley said. "In Saskatoon."

"Well, I'm impressed," Deutsch said, then turned to Andy.

"Ever hear of Cramdon before?"

"Can't say I have."

"He's the biggest, meanest, sharpest lawyer going," Grenfell said. "You know what I mean? You got them down your way, too? The real smart lawyers?"

"You mean the ones guilty guys hire?" Andy said, picking up the cue.

"That's the kind I mean," Grenfell said, with a nasty smile.

"By all means give him a call, when you get home," Deutsch said. "He'll explain that you've got nothing to worry about because we haven't charged you with anything. But tell him we might want to have another little chat with you in the next few days. He'll tell you what to do."

"Can I go now?" Rowley asked.

"Sure," Deutsch said, then called for Constable Resnick, who came into the room a few seconds later.

"Dewey, can you give Mr. Rowley a ride home?"

"Yes, sir."

"Great, that's just great," Deutsch said. "And maybe you'd just keep an eye on the house tonight. Know what I mean?"

"Yes, sir."

"All right, then, off you go, Mr. Rowley. Thanks for all your help."

Rowley, got up, looking confused. Just as he got to the door, Deutsch called to him.

"Mr. Rowley, you drive a pickup truck, don't you?"

"Yes, why?"

"Just asking. Have a nice evening."

The three policemen watched in silence until the suspect was out of the building.

"What do you think?" Deutsch asked.

"He's starting to sweat," Grenfell said.

"You give terrific bad cop, by the way," Andy said.

"Hey, what about my good cop?" Deutsch asked.

"Excellent, as well."

"Compliments aside, what's your read on the guy?"

"He's worth watching. What did you find out on his alibis?"

"Two of them weren't home yet, but Banjo Rasmussen confirms he was dropped off last, around ten to one."

"Which doesn't mean Rowley went right home," Andy said. "One o'clock was when Virna Wilton was seen leaving the bar. He could have been back at the hotel by then."

"His aunt says she heard him come in," Grenfell added. "I talked to her before the kid got home. Only she says it was 12:30. They didn't have time to get their stories straight."

"Anything else at the house?"

"I looked at his room. There was an old autographed baseball there. Like the ones they have at the Hall of Fame."

"Could be a trophy, like the things he took from those women's houses before," Andy said.

"He says it was his late father's."

"Check it out in the morning," Deutsch said. "He's the best suspect we've got."

CHAPTER

29

I showered, put on jeans and a clean tee-shirt, then headed downstairs, looking for some company to cheer me up. I met Mrs. Deneka in the lobby, heading for the front door. She stopped when she saw me.

"What time does the bus get here?"

"Which bus?"

"The bus to the ballpark," she said, impatiently. "We've got a game tonight and the bus isn't here."

"I didn't know about the game," I stalled, looking around for her husband. "I thought you were having dinner with my parents and Edna."

"They're in the dining room, pretending there isn't a game. They're going to get in trouble."

"Did you mention it to them?" I asked.

"No, I just remembered now, when I was in the Ladies' Room."

"Why don't we go and tell them?" I asked, taking her gently by the arm and steering her towards the restaurant.

"But the bus might come," she said, pulling away from me. She was surprisingly strong. "I can't miss the bus."

"They won't leave without you," I said.

"That Virna will make them," she said. "She wants to get me in trouble again."

"I'll make sure you don't miss it," I said.

I held open the restaurant door for her.

"I'd drive my own car, but someone took away my keys," she said, stepping into the restaurant.

Peter Deneka got up from the table, smiling, when he saw us, and crossed the room.

"We were wondering where you'd got to," he said. "We were about to send out a search party."

I wasn't sure how to handle the situation. Diplomacy is not my strength, and I was afraid of appearing condescending.

"Your wife was wondering about a bus," I tried. "To go to the ballpark."

He understood at once, and looked at her with a heartbreaking combination of love and sadness.

"There's no bus, Meg. And no ballpark. That was all over years ago."

He took her hand and led her back to the table, after smiling his thanks to me. I watched them go, then went back into the lobby.

I went into Shooters and found Jack Wilton sitting at the bar, alone, where we had been on Saturday night, less than forty-eight hours before. I joined him and lit a cigarette. He took one too.

"I'm not very good company," he said.

"I don't expect you to be. Would you rather be alone?"

"No. I appreciate having someone to talk to. I'm sick of sitting here with my own thoughts."

"If there's anything I can do, just ask."

"I just finished talking to my kids, telling them about their grandmother. It wasn't easy."

"How many children do you have?"

"Two, a boy and a girl. They're teenagers now."

"Were they close to their grandmother?"

"Not really, to tell you the truth, which is mostly my fault."

"How so?"

"There was a time in my life when I didn't see much of her and Wilma, when my children were young."

"Why is that?"

"It's a long story."

"I haven't any immediate plans," I said.

"Well, growing up, all I could think about was getting out of Fort Wayne. I wanted a different life. After I did my time in Vietnam, I went to the University of Chicago. I got my M.B.A. in 1975, then stayed in Chicago, got married to the rich and beautiful daughter of a major manufacturer, and worked my way up his corporate ladder, rung by rung. We had the nice house in the suburbs, membership at the golf club, the whole nine yards. I had reinvented myself into the high-powered big-city guy I thought I wanted to be. And there was no place in my new life for my Mom and Aunt Wilma, I am now ashamed to say."

"They wouldn't have fit in at the country club?"

"Not hardly. Mom could have maybe passed, but not Aunt Wilma. And certainly not the two of them together."

He smiled.

"Beth never really liked them, either. They embarrassed her. Both of us, to be truthful. And her parents could barely bring themselves to be civil the few times they met. But Mom and Wilma didn't care. I'm just thankful I came home in time to enjoy some good years with them."

His smile turned rueful, and his eyes misted over.

"At least I had that."

I looked away while he wiped the tears.

"Are you okay?" I asked after a moment.

"Yeah. I'm fine. Anyway, that's the story of why Megan and John Junior weren't close to their grandmother Wilton."

"You said that it was the life you thought you wanted. What changed that? What brought you back to Fort Wayne and the flower shop?"

"Well, on my fortieth birthday, right in the middle of a big black-tie bash she threw for me at the club, I realized that I was deeply unhappy. The old mid-life thing."

"Don't tell me, you bought a red sports car."

He laughed.

"That one I didn't do. Younger women, I did. I finally left home when I was forty-three to live in a downtown loft with a beautiful, successful, young woman who worked in public relations."

"And your wife?"

"Took me for everything she could. Not that I blame her. Anyhow, within a couple of years, I was sick of hanging out in jazz clubs until four in the morning listening to a bunch of thirty-somethings talking about target markets. By then, of course, Beth had remarried. I went back to Fort Wayne for Christmas that year, for the first time in ages. It was fun being with Mom and Aunt Wilma, and I realized that I felt like I had come home. To my real home. When Mom suggested I come into the business, it made sense. They were both getting on, and there was room for some innovative expansion in the business."

"And it's worked out?"

"It's worked out great. Better than I ever expected, or deserved, probably. I don't miss Chicago, or the stress of success. Maybe I'm just defining success differently. I don't make as much money as I used to, but I get by better on less. I've been dating a woman my age, and that's looking good. She's divorced, too, with a couple of kids who are almost grown. So, I'm learning to be a family man again. Maybe for the first time. I guess, touch wood, I've found a bit of happiness. Finally."

A cloud crossed his face.

"Well, I guess I wouldn't say happy, right now."

"But you've found what you need in life."

"Rhonda, the woman I'm seeing now, was someone I dated for a while in high school. So I've kind of come full circle."

"Starting over?"

"Maybe I won't screw up so bad this time around."

He finished his drink and signalled to the bartender.

"Another one?"

"I'm still fine. Speaking of high-school sweethearts, did you know that your Aunt Wilma was once engaged to Morley Timms?"

"No, I didn't. Morley Timms? You're kidding."

"Evidently. I was doing some research at the Hall of Fame and saw it in her files."

"Well, if I did know, I'd forgotten. Morley Timms. Do you think that's why they called our old dog Morley?"

"Could be."

"I'm glad I didn't mention it to him, then," he laughed.

"I talked to a woman at the museum who knew Morley and Garth and Wilma in the old days."

I told him the story of what Morley's war had done to him.

"Man, that's sad. There's a lot of drama tied up in all these old people," he said.

"I know. The older I get the more I realize that everybody's got history that's really interesting. Wilma's life is the stuff of a novel. So was your mother's."

"And your mother's, too."

"Maybe a novella," I laughed. "A slim volume. Aside from the five years she spent playing ball, she's led a pretty dull life."

"And now my mother's has turned into a detective story," Jack said, bitterly.

"What do you remember about Garth Elshaw from when you were a kid? I was talking to him yesterday and he said that you used to be close but you'd lost touch over the years."

"Yeah, well. I feel kind of bad about that. We came up every summer for a while, to Wilma's family's cabin. For four or five years, maybe. The summer I was thirteen, when I wasn't getting on too well at home, I came up by myself for the whole summer. It was great. He spent a lot of time with me, let me work with the animals on the farm and everything. Looking back, I really appreciate it. He was my main father-figure then. The only man in my life. But you know what happens. Once I became a teenager, being cool was all that mattered, and there's nothing cool about a Saskatchewan farm. No offence."

"None taken. I ran away from home too."

There was a commotion over by the door, an outburst of laughter. I looked across the room to see Andy coming in the lounge with Sergeant Deutsch of the Mounties, clearly enjoying a joke. When they saw Jack sitting there, they had the good grace to look embarrassed.

CHAPTER

30

After the two policemen joined us, we all moved to a corner table. Sergeant Deutsch wanted some privacy to speak with Jack about developments in the investigation, and the bar was starting to fill up. Andy told me I could sit in if I promised to keep my mouth shut.

"We have found a pretty solid suspect," Deutsch said.

"You've arrested somebody?" Jack asked.

"No, we haven't got enough evidence to do that yet, but we've got a direction to look at now. This is a guy who has been in jail before for roughing up elderly women. The pattern matches. He was here in this bar the night she died, and acknowledges having spoken to her."

"And you just let him go?"

"We can't hold him without charging him, and we aren't ready to do that yet. He's being watched carefully. He won't go anywhere without our knowing about it."

"What's this guy's name?" Jack asked.

"I don't want to reveal that at this time, Mr. Wilton. We're checking his alibi, which has got some holes in it, and he is consulting his lawyer. We'll be questioning him again tomorrow."

"Is there any connection with the Hall of Fame?" I asked.

"Yes, there is," Deutsch said. "He would have been aware of the location of the key, for example."

"But what about the letters?" I asked, ignoring Andy's look of annoyance. "Can you tie those letters to him?"

"There has always been a possibility that the letters and the murder are not connected," Deutsch said. "It's just a coincidence."

"What did this guy say when you asked him about the murder?" Jack asked.

"Just that we got the wrong guy," Deutsch said.

"Penitentiaries are full of wrong guys," Andy said, sarcastically, "every one of them convicted by a jury of his peers."

"My gut tells me he's the one," Deutsch said.

"I thought you didn't listen to your gut," I said.

"I think what I said was that gut feelings aren't evidence," he corrected me. "But in this case we have opportunity, proximity, and past behaviour to go on. The rest is just connecting the dots."

"And in the meantime he's walking free," Jack said.

"In the meantime, he has Constable Resnick on his ass so tight he'll have to ask his permission to take a shit, if you'll pardon my language."

He put his empty beer glass down.

"You say this man was in jail," I said. "Is he on parole? Can't you lock him up for violating his parole?"

"The thought did occur to us," Deutsch said. "But that isn't our decision, it's his parole officer's, and he doesn't appear to have done anything that violates it."

"Except for murdering my mother," Jack burst out. "The minor matter of murdering a fine woman doesn't count, I guess."

He wound down and stared at the table as if he could see the crime enacted on its scarred Formica top. The veins on his neck stood out, and he gripped his glass so hard his hand was white across the knuckles. I reached over and took it from him. He looked up, startled.

"I know it's difficult," I said, "but they're right."

He just stared into my eyes while the anger drained from his face, to be replaced by a kind of helpless despair. I gave him back his glass, and he drained it in one gulp.

"We're going to get something to eat," I said. "Do you want to join us?"

"No, I think I'll just stick to my malt diet," he said.

"That's not the answer, Jack."

"And what was the question?"

"Kate, I think Jack wants to spend some time alone," Andy said. Jack looked at him gratefully. There was a slightly awkward silence, then we got up from the table. Andy went to the bar to sign the bill to our room. Deutsch and I went ahead out into the lobby.

"Where are we going to eat?" I asked.

"It depends on what kind of food you like."

I knew it was useless in the Battlefords to suggest anything other than Italian, Chinese, or Canadian, whatever that means.

"Take us to your favourite place."

"My girlfriend's house? I don't think she'd appreciate it."

"I don't really care, as long as it's not here."

"You like steak?"

"Sure."

"I know a good place."

Andy also thought a hunk of cow would do the trick, so we headed out, with Don Deutsch driving. The restaurant, in a small strip mall in North Battleford, was unassuming in appearance, but the meat was good, and they had a passable house wine. We mostly made small talk while we ate, but afterwards, satisfied and relaxed, the two cops loosened up a bit.

"Something interesting came out of the autopsy report," Andy said to me. "You might be interested to know that Virna Wilton had a medical condition that made it impossible for her to conceive a child."

"What do you mean?"

"I forget the medical term for it, but she didn't have a uterus. I'm no expert on these things, but it seems to me that it's kind of hard to have a child without one."

"Holy smokes. So Jack isn't her son?"

"It's so good to see your keen investigative mind at work."

"Shut up. I wonder where the baby came from?"

"Maybe the stork brought it," Don said.

"That's very interesting," I said. "I'm going to have to dig around a bit. Maybe Jack is really Wilma's."

"I'm sure you'll ferret out the answer one way or another," Andy said.

"What else did the autopsy show?" I asked. Perhaps emboldened by the wine. "How did she die?"

"She was hit on the head, probably by a baseball bat, then strangled with something like a scarf," Deutsch said. "But keep that confidential. We haven't let that information out."

"I can be trusted with a confidence," I said. "Tell him, Andy."

"I have to admit it, she can."

"You know I can," I said. "And you know something else? I think you guys are on the wrong track."

"Here she goes again," Andy groaned.

"I still say the letters are important. If you can't tie your suspect to the letters, you've got the wrong man."

"Look, I can't pretend I'm not bothered by the letters," Deutsch said. "But it is possible, you know, that this is a separate matter. We know that people who write these things don't usually follow through."

"Yes, but it's not just the letters that bother me," I said. "It's the whole Hall of Fame connection that seems to be missing. It just seems too weird to me that these women get together for the first time in all these years and one of them ends up, not only dead, but dead in the Hall of Fame that was their connection."

"We know she wanted to go to the Hall to play some sort of practical joke," Deutsch said. "Let's suppose she asked this guy, a local, if he could help her. That's possible. Or maybe he overheard her talking about it. Anyway, he dropped off his buddies and came back and picked her up. It's possible."

"Other people are more likely to have had some old secret reason to want her dead," I insisted.

"For God's sake, Kate, who do you think did it?" Andy asked, angrily. "Your mother? Or your father? Did Edna

Summers with her arthritic knees just up and strangle Virna Wilton with a silk scarf and then go around doing her own investigation just to confuse us? Or Mrs. Goodman, all twisted up the way she is? Maybe poor old Mrs. Deneka, who barely knows her own name, did it."

"I know it sounds stupid," I admitted.

"Leave the investigation to the professionals," Andy said. "In case I've never told you that before."

"Well, I hope you wrap this up soon," I said. "I'm ready to get out of this place and go back home. Nothing personal, Don."

"Yeah, you Toronto people panic if you're away from your cappuccino machines for too long," he said, with a smile.

"Right," I said. "Fresh air and friendly people get us all twitchy and belligerent."

"It's the politeness drives me crazy," Andy said. "No one has given me the finger in days."

I flipped him one. He sighed and slumped back in his chair.

"Thanks, I needed that," he said.

CHAPTER

31

Next morning, I had breakfast alone. After our night on the town with Don Deutsch, and some private shenanigans back at the hotel, we slept in, and Andy only had time to grab a quick coffee before rushing off to the police station. My parents, of course, had long since finished eating.

I was just digging into my bacon and eggs when Garth Elshaw appeared. I put down my newspaper and asked him to join me.

"Just for a moment," he said, twisting his baseball cap in his hands nervously. "I'm meeting someone."

"Have a coffee with me, anyway. I hate eating alone."

He sat down and the waitress appeared instantly with the coffee pot.

"You want breakfast?"

"Just coffee."

She left and silence fell on the table. I felt awkward eating while he sat twisting his hat.

"What's the weather like?" I asked.

"Raining again. They say there's going to be four centimetres."

"Good for the farmers."

"Yep."

"And for the ducks," I said. "But if you don't happen to be a farmer or a duck, it can be a bit of a pain."

He made a sound that might have been a laugh.

"You know, Mr. Elshaw, Jack Wilton was talking to me just last night about the things you did together when he was growing up without a father. He hasn't forgotten."

"That's who I'm here to see," he said, pushing his glasses up the bridge of his nose.

"I'm glad to hear that."

"Well, I was just going to let it go, but Morley told me to call him up and see if we can patch things up between us."

"You were wise to listen to Morley, then."

"Morley's not dumb, you know," he said, then stopped, as if embarrassed.

"I was told a bit about it yesterday. Someone who knew him said he was a real live-wire before the war and came back a changed man. Is that true?"

"We saw some terrible things over there," he said, cryptically. "Some fellows take it harder than others."

"All his plans for the future changed, too," I continued, probing. "Including his marriage plans to your sister."

"Where did you hear about that?"

"I read it in one of the articles at the Hall of Fame."

"Oh, I see." He shifted uncomfortably in his chair.

"Well, yes," he finally said. "But you couldn't blame her for cancelling it, the way he was when he came back."

"I thought it was the other way around."

"Who have you been talking to?"

"I don't want to get anybody in trouble."

"Well, it was the other way, at first. Morley thought he would be a burden. When he got better, it was too late. She'd taken up with that Wilton woman."

"But you still had them up here for the summer holidays, didn't you?"

"Well, Wilma was my sister. And Maude, that was my late wife, invited her. I went along with it for the sake of the boy."

He paused, then reddened.

"But I made sure they slept in separate bedrooms when they came to us."

"I don't think that's really any of my business," I said.

"Looks like you're making it your business, reading all those old stories and talking to any busybody in town with gossip to spread."

"I'm sorry, Mr. Elshaw, if I've offended you. I didn't mean to pry. I just wanted to write an article about the wonderful accomplishments of the women in the All-American Girls Professional League."

"Excuse me, Miss Henry. I was out of line. But you just be careful what you write. There are some pots best left unstirred."

"I'll remember that," I said, then saw Jack Wilton come into the room. He raised his hand in greeting and came to our table.

"Good morning," he said. "I'm sorry I'm late."

"That's fine," I said. "I said. "Mr. Elshaw and I have been having a nice chat.".

Elshaw stood up. And, after a slightly awkward pause, the two of them made their way to a table across the room. I went back to my paper. I also kept an eye on the meeting between the two men.

It was a classic: two men trying to cross an emotional chasm without the tools to build the bridge. Women would have hugged, but they had to make do with words, a medium in which at least one of them was not comfortable. Garth sat stiffly, looking down at his coffee cup while Jack talked earnestly to the top of his head. Finally, he reached over and touched Garth tentatively on the arm. The "uncle" raised his head. Jack smiled. Some of the stiffness went out of Garth's body, and he laughed. Then they both were talking. Not easily, yet, there were still long pauses, and eyes that didn't quite meet, but I left the restaurant knowing that the first steps had been taken.

I found my parents by the pool. My mother was knitting and my father was reading a book.

"If you don't watch out, you'll find that idleness suits you," I teased.

"There is visible labour and invisible labour," my father said, looking over the tops of his glasses. "Victor Hugo. 'A man is not idle if he is absorbed in thought.' I, my dear, am absorbed in thought. Your mother, as usual, is absorbed in good works, knitting for the United Church Women Christmas sale."

"Only 117 knitting days left," I joked. She smiled, vaguely.

"We missed you at breakfast this morning," Daddy said.

"We slept in, I'm afraid. It's been a busy few days."

"You haven't been idle, then."

"I'm still working on the article about the league, Mum. I'm going through the files, and I want to interview you."

"I don't think so, dear," she said. "My story isn't very interesting."

"Of course it is," I said. "You were all so daring to leave your small towns, to go so far away and do something so adventurous. Seeing you all together this weekend has really made me realize that. I'd love to talk to you about it. Please?"

My mother looked quite surprised.

"Well, I suppose so, if you like," she said. "When would you like to talk? Right now?"

"Well, actually, I'd like to go back to the Hall of Fame this morning, if I can borrow the car, and finish what I started yesterday. Maybe after lunch."

"Where's your car?"

"Andy took it to the RCMP detachment. They seem to have found a local suspect to question."

"I certainly hope they've found the man," my father said.

"Yes, and that there was no connection with anything from back then," my mother said. "I must confess, I found it very uncomfortable to think it might be someone we knew."

"Well, I've been feeling like a prisoner," my father said, "stuck here in the hotel, with everybody afraid to go anywhere."

"Where is the rest of the crew this morning?" I asked. "Edna and the Denekas."

"Edna is sitting with Meg in her room," my mother said. "Poor Peter had some things he had to do, and didn't want to leave her alone. She needs looking after." She sighed.

"I hope that doesn't happen to me."

"It's strange how she can be quite with-it one moment, then get lost in another time," I said.

"Well, Peter says it's gradually getting worse. This wandering has just started recently. Poor Meg. I feel for her."

"Well, touch wood everything's all right so far," I said, tapping my knuckles lightly on my father's head.

He smiled up at me.

"Can I have the keys then? I'll come back at lunchtime."

My mother opened her purse and handed them to me.

"Drive carefully," my father said, as he has done every time I have left him for almost thirty years.

The rain hadn't let up. I stopped at the Petro-Canada station for a fill-up and bought a Pepsi to drink while I worked. I got to the Hall of Fame just after ten. There was an old pickup truck parked out front. I went around back for the key, but it wasn't on the hiding hook. Swearing under my breath, I went to the front door and tried it. It was unlocked. I pushed it open and stepped inside.

I didn't see anyone at first, but the lights were on. I was about to call out when I saw the legs. There was a body sprawled on the floor on the very spot where Virna Wilton's had been found, this one with the head and torso jammed under the organ's keyboard.

CHAPTER

32

I didn't scream, but I probably gasped. Rushing across the room, I managed to knock over a mannequin, which crashed to the floor. In response to all this commotion, the corpse began to move. The feet twitched first, then the legs. Then, slowly, it slid out from under the organ and revealed itself to be the very alive Morley Timms.

"Mr. Timms, you scared me half to death," I said. "I thought you were, well, never mind what I thought. What on earth are you doing there?"

He began to laugh, showing the gaps in his back teeth. He had a high-pitched giggle.

"You thought I was a goner, eh? That's a good one. Wait'll I tell Garth."

I began to laugh, too, giddy with relief.

"I was just trying to get ahold of this," he said, holding out some sort of knob. I took it and could see it was one of the stops from the organ.

"Things got a bit messed up here, I guess you'd say, and Dave Shury asked me to come in to tidy up and fix anything that needed it."

He pointed to one of the display cases.

"See, I replaced the glass there, where it got cracked, and I'm cleaning up the mess those police left."

"That's a lot of work," I said. "I hope I won't be in your way over here."

"I'll be glad of the company," he said. "It was a bit spooky in here alone. Creepy-crawly."

"I know what you mean. I was working here yesterday, and every time I heard a noise, I jumped out of my skin."

"Probably just the mice," he said. "There are some around. Church mice. No one told them that it's not a church any more."

"Maybe it's a new breed. Hall of Fame mice."

"Famous fame mice," he giggled.

I sat down and opened a new box of files.

"I'd better get to work," I said.

"They got the guy, you know," Morley said, hanging around the desk. "The one who killed Virna."

Clearly, the whole town knew about the suspect.

"That man shouldn't have been let out of jail, you know," Morley continued. "They should have thrown away the key. A man like that who beats up old women, they should string him up by the necktie."

I made noncommittal *hmm*ing noises in my throat, opened another file and opened my notebook. I didn't feel like opening up a capital punishment debate with Morley Timms.

"Are you writing a story about the museum?"

"Well, not really. More about the women's baseball league."

"You should write about the museum," he said.

"Maybe I will some day. Now I'd really better get to work."

He took the hint, and got back underneath the organ, his round bum stuck comically in the air. I began going through the files and scrapbooks of the Saskatchewan women who had played for other teams. In the early days, much was made of these exotics from the frozen north. One woman, the league president claimed, travelled to Saskatoon by dog sled to catch the train for spring training in Chicago. Added to the geographical stereotypes were the sexual ones, unintentionally hilarious with forty years' worth of hindsight. I particularly liked the picture of a catcher, with her mask pulled up on her head, looking into her compact mirror while powdering her nose.

I scribbled notes happily, knowing that I had the angle which would amuse the readers while honouring the women of the league and their real accomplishments.

While I worked, Morley Timms pottered around, whistling tunelessly under his breath. From time to time I would look up and catch him staring at me. Then he'd flash a goofy grin and start looking busy. I thought about the stories Gladys Bieber had told me about him in his youth, when he was a charming heartbreaker. I could see traces of it in that smile.

After about half an hour, I put down my pen and stretched. I opened my Pepsi, which was still cold, drank some.

"Sorry I didn't know you were here, Mr. Timms. I would have brought you a cold drink too."

"Never mind about that," he said, straightening up from the cabinet he had been rearranging. "And you don't have to call me Mr. Timms, either. Just call me Morley, like everybody else."

"All right, Morley. Do you do a lot of work for the museum?"

"There's always something that needs being done. Fixing things up, running errands for Mr. Shury, going to the post office and things like that."

"You must be a baseball fan, then."

"Lifelong."

"Did you ever play?"

"I was captain of the Battleford team back before the war. It was a good one, too. Crackerjack. I'll show you a picture."

He led me to a wall covered in framed photos and pointed.

"See, I'm in the Hall of Fame, too," he said, proudly.

It wasn't a very big picture. A faded ink inscription indicated that the Battleford Mounties were Prairie League Champions in 1941. I looked more closely, but couldn't recognize Morley Timms, there being no egg-shaped old men in the picture. I asked him for help, and he pointed to the player in the centre of the front row, hat off and grinning, in contrast to his more serious team-mates. Then he pointed to another player, a tall, handsome man in the second row.

"That there's Garth Elshaw," he said. "Centre fielder."

"What position did you play?"

He pointed to himself and laughed.

"Shortstop, what do you think?"

"I bet you were good," I said. "And after the war, did you play again?"

"I wasn't in such good health," he said, uncomfortably. "But we played overseas, Garth and I. We showed those English a thing or two. We even played on board our ship. Except every time someone hit a home run, the ball would end up in the drink."

He laughed merrily at the thought.

"Well, it's too bad you had to give it up. I bet it brought you a lot of pleasure."

"Nothing to be done about it."

"And Garth Elshaw? Did he play afterwards?"

"No. He coached some, is all."

"Wilma was an outfielder like her brother, wasn't she?"

"Garth and me, we taught Wilma to play."

"You were good teachers, then," I said. "I wish I'd known her. She sounds like a remarkable woman."

I watched him for a response, but aside from a small sigh, he didn't reveal anything.

"She was the best I ever saw," he said. "Best woman, anyways."

He turned away from me abruptly.

"I have to get back to work," he said. I stayed and looked at the photo for awhile, then hung it back on the wall and went back to the desk. I dug out Wilma's files and Virna's scrapbooks. I found the newspaper clipping about the flower shop and put it on the desk, then pulled out the article about Wilma from her file. Morley had filled a pail with suds and was busy mopping the floor. I waited until he came close to the library area.

"I was just reading this article about Wilma," I said. "It says that you and she were engaged to be married."

He kept mopping, in slow, thoughtful circles.

"That was a long time ago," he finally said. "Lot of water under the bridge since then."

"I guess she had her career."

"We were both different when I got back," he said.

He smiled then.

"I guess we weren't neither of us the marrying kind," he said.

"Did you keep in touch?"

"Never saw her again."

"But I thought she came back to visit Garth and his family in the summers."

"Didn't visit me."

He kept mopping the same section of the floor with a vehemence inappropriate to the task. It suddenly struck me that he was mopping the place where Virna had been found, as if to clean the stain away.

"You're going to wear yourself out, Morley," I said. "Or wear out the floor."

He stopped swabbing and looked at me.

"I guess you learned your technique in the navy," I said, trying to lighten the mood. "Swabbing those decks, I mean."

"Maybe," he said. "A lot of the fellows hated it, but I never did mind. I'd just sing a song, maybe, just in my head. I think it's kind of restful. Calming, like."

"I know what you mean. I feel the same way about ironing."

"Ironing. I like that too. I like keeping things nice."

"A lot of people spend a lot of money to get that calm.

If everyone ironed instead, the psychiatrists would all go broke."

That set him off. He laughed his high-pitched giggle and began to mop again.

"Psychiatrists would all go broke. Ha!"

I realized it was time to join my parents for lunch. I folded up my notebook and got up.

"I have to go now. I have an appointment. But I'd like to leave these papers out for later. Think they'll be safe?"

"Won't bother me," he said.

"Well, maybe I'll see you later. If not, I know where to get the key."

"Okey-dokey."

"It's been nice talking to you."

"Same here, Miss Henry. It's been a pleasure."

"That's not fair. If I call you Morley, you have to call me Kate."

"Okey-dokey, Kate."

As I let myself out the door, I could hear him singing the song my father used to sing to me, "K-k-k-katie, my beautiful Katie." Smiling, I stepped back into the wind and rain.

I had just got into my car when Ruth Fernie pulled up next to me in her station wagon. She put on her emergency brake, then scooted across the front seat and signalled for me to roll down my window.

"Please, Miss Henry, can I talk to you for a minute? I don't know where else to turn."

CHAPTER

33

Rather than get both of us wet, I got out of my car and got into Ruth Fernie's.

"I'm so glad I found you," she said. "I was just driving around trying to figure out what to do when I saw you. It was like a sign."

"What's the matter?"

"It's my nephew, Nathan Rowley," she said. "The police think he's the one who killed Mrs. Wilton. They have him at the police station right now."

"Your nephew's been arrested?"

"He's there at the police station again this morning. But he never did it, I promise you."

"I wish I could help, Mrs. Fernie, but I don't see how."

"You can talk to your friend the policeman and tell him about Nat. How he's not the same as when he did those crimes before. He learned his lesson."

She began to cry.

"I just don't know what to do. He's all I've got. My late husband and I never had any children. Nat was my sister's boy. She died when he was a teenager. Her husband shot her, then took his own life. After that Nat went wild. But now he's settled down and is a good boy. I know it."

"Did you talk to the police? Tell them this?"

"Yes, but I just got him into more trouble."

"How?"

"They asked me if I heard him come home that night, and I said yes. Then they asked me what time, and I said the wrong time. I said half past twelve and he told them one o'clock."

"So you didn't really hear him."

"No, I was asleep," she said. "But I believe him when he says he didn't do it. He wouldn't lie to me."

"I think you should get him a lawyer, right away," I said.

"He has one. From before. He drove out from Saskatoon this morning."

"Then you can be sure that his rights are being protected," I said. "Another thing you can do is find some other people who can vouch for him. Like his employer, or your minister."

Giving her a project was the most helpful thing I could think of. It took her mind off her fears and gave her something to occupy herself. I promised her I would pass on her messages to Andy when I saw him and got back into my own car for the drive back to the hotel.

My parents and Edna were waiting for me in the lobby. Despite the weather, I suggested an outing to the place Deutsch had taken us to the night before, just to combat everybody's cabin fever.

"A capital idea," my father said. "A new menu is just what the doctor ordered."

"Where are the Denekas?" I asked. "Should we invite them, too?"

"I don't think so," Edna said, quietly. "Meg isn't up to it today. He ordered food up to the room."

After a certain commotion with umbrellas and discussion about who would drive and whether or not Edna would need her walker or just her cane, we got the show on the road. There was a table just finishing when we got to the restaurant. By the time we had ordered, we were all feeling a bit more cheerful than we had in days.

Probably so that mood wouldn't end, no one brought up the murder or the investigation. I led the conversation back to the old days of the All-American Girls. All I had to do was ask a couple of questions and my mother and Edna were unstoppable for the next hour. With Edna's prompting, my mother loosened up and told some of the stories that hadn't made it into the official histories.

"Remember the time in Fort Wayne when we kept Max Humphreys up all night in the lobby?" Edna asked, and they both laughed.

"He was the manager that year, and no one liked him," my mother explained. "He was very strict about curfew. Two hours after the game his girls had to be tucked into bed. So one night some of us went to get something to eat after the game, and when we got back, we could see that he was sitting in the lobby watching the door."

"Meg put us up to this," Edna interrupted. "We sneaked around to the fire escape at the back of the hotel and got in that way. He waited all night to catch us coming in."

"In the morning, we just waltzed down to breakfast," my mother said, "and there was nothing he could do. He was some mad. And the funniest thing was, we hadn't even missed curfew. We were back well before time."

"Oh, we had some good times," Edna said.

"What kind of money did you make?" I asked.

"The starting salary was fifty-five dollars a week," Edna said. "And believe it or not, that was darned good pay back then."

"Easy for you to say," my mother said. "Sluggers like you could supplement it. The rest of us had to make do."

"What do you mean?" Andy asked.

"Oh, nothing illegal," Edna said. "After a home run, I would run down the first-base line shaking hands with the fans, and darned if there wouldn't be a little folding green in some of the hands. But I always shared, didn't I, Helen. Be honest."

"That's true. Edna was always kind with her tips. She'd buy beer for the rest of us back at the rooming-house."

"I thought drinking and smoking were forbidden," I said.

"In public, sure. But no one had to know what went on in the rooming-house," Edna said. "Including, by the way, what your mother isn't telling you, which is how she made her extra money."

She paused for effect.

"At the card table. Helen was the best poker player in the whole darned league."

I looked at my mother, stunned. She smiled.

"Well, I was pretty good," she admitted.

"Virna, too," Edna said. "They used to clean out all the rookies on pay day, until the chaperone got wise to it."

"After that, we had to keep the money off the table and pretend we were playing rummy if the chaperone came in," my mother said. "And we didn't gamble any more with anyone who couldn't afford to lose."

"Now I find out my lady wife was a card shark," my father laughed. "If I'd known, I could have sent you to Las Vegas once a year to supplement the parish income."

"Oh, those were good times," Edna said. I'd give anything to go back. Wouldn't you, Helen? Back to when everything was a big adventure."

"Oh, I don't know," she said, then smiled at my father. "I've had a good life since then, too."

I looked at my watch.

"I should get you all back to the hotel so I can get in a couple more hours at the Hall of Fame and finish the piece I'm writing for the weekend. These stories were just what I needed. Now all I need to do is fill in some of the stats."

"We're glad to help," Edna said. "Just don't forget to send me a copy."

"I won't. I bet you could help me solve another little mystery I'm working on, too. Just out of my own curiosity."

"What's that?" Edna asked.

"Who Jack Wilton's parents are."

"What do you mean?" my mother asked. "Virna was his mother, and his father was killed during the war."

"Oh, Helen, you always were so naive," Edna said.

221

I told them what the autopsy report had said.

"Well, well," Edna said. "I must say, I always had my suspicions."

"Do you think he could have been Wilma's son?" I asked.

"Wouldn't that be something?" Edna asked, clearly intrigued. "But wait a minute. She wasn't close to Virna until after the baby appeared. Those first few years – I remember because we were rookies together in '44 – that year Wilma was friends with what's her name, Marilyn Dyck from Manitoba. Remember, Helen? So that can't be it."

"Well, I don't think it's any of our business anyway," my mother said. "With both Virna and Wilma passed away, that secret's gone to the grave. I think we should leave it there."

"Oh, I'll figure it out, Mother," I said. "That's what I do best."

CHAPTER

34

When I got back to the Hall of Fame, it was locked up tight, and the key was back on its hook. Once inside, I left my raincoat to drip by the front door and went back to the desk. Everything was as I had left it, with one exception. I had left Virna's scrapbook open to the article about the flower shop. Someone had taken a ballpoint pen and scribbled over the picture of Virna and Wilma with an angry-looking scrawl.

I checked the rest of the files and nothing was missing. There had been two people around when I left the museum earlier: Ruth Fernie and Morley Timms. Mrs. Fernie had more pressing things to concern her than an old clipping. It had to be Morley. At least he might know something about it.

I found the phonebook and looked up his address. My tourist map showed me that his house wasn't far away. In Battleford, nothing is far away. I locked up, then took a drive.

He lived on 16th street, on the edge of town in a sort of jumped-up trailer park. All the trailers were grounded, set in small yards on paved streets. There were air conditioners sticking out of most of the units. It was nicer than a trailer park, more permanent, but it was as if it was only pretending to be a neighbourhood.

I went up the path to Morley's door past neatly tended flowerbeds filled with brightly coloured nasturtiums.

I knocked on the door. Nothing happened at first, but I saw a sheer curtain move at the window, and Morley's face peered out. I waved and smiled, and a moment later he opened the door. What hair he had was ruffled as if he had just got out of bed.

"My goodness, I'm sorry to keep you standing out here in the rain," he said. "I couldn't imagine who it was."

He fussed as I came through the door.

"I don't get many visitors, and those that do come don't knock," he said.

His living room was amazing, crammed full of more stuff than I had ever seen before, things, objects, doodads, all arranged in an obsessively tidy fashion. Shelves covered three of the four walls, well-built shelves that held collections of what to others might be junk, here treated with the respect usually reserved for precious art.

"I could make some coffee," Morley suggested, breaking an awkward silence. "Or tea. Would you like some tea?"

"I'd love a cup of tea, if it's not too much trouble."

"I'll put on the kettle," Morley said. "You just make yourself to home."

224

I looked around. A faded brown corduroy reclining chair sat directly across the room from the television set. A radio was playing on the shelf next to it, and a reading lamp stood beside it. It was obviously Morley's favourite. A loveseat upholstered in a yellowish plaid fabric clashed with the moss-coloured shag carpeting. There were also a desk and chair. I wandered around the room, looking at his things, looking for clues to Morley Timms's peculiar life.

There was a three-shelf library: Pierre Bertons, military histories, and novels set in the old west, arranged in alphabetical order. There were no records or CDs or, at a glance, anything to play them on. Each shelf seemed to have a theme. One held a box full of tickets to sporting events, arranged chronologically since 1947; back issues of the *Saskatchewan Historical Baseball Review*; and an old-fashioned glove, clumsy and overpadded. God knows how anyone caught a ball with one of those things. A photocopy of the picture Morley had shown me at the museum earlier, the one of the Battleford Mounties, was tacked to the wall behind the shelf.

Continuing the sporting motif in the next shelf was a tackle box full of lures, leaders, lead weights, and fishing line. Old fishing and hunting licences were stacked in a neat pile. Photos of him with Garth Elshaw and a dead deer, ditto with dead geese and dead fish. A curling trophy from 1979. I saw his broom propped in a corner, next to a shotgun.

I moved to the next section, nearest to the desk, which was full of stationery supplies: pens and pencils held together in bundles with elastic bands; a box of paperclips and those brass doohickeys you poke through holes in paper and bend back; a plastic container of thumb-tacks and push-pins; a pad of pink message slips; a stapler sitting between a box of staples and a staple remover; a stack of empty used file folders and a box of labels. A three-drawer filing cabinet stood next to the door. I looked at it longingly, but I could hear the kettle whistling in the kitchen. I looked back at the shelf, then picked up a bundle of marking pens and ballpoints, in a whole range of colours from ordinary black and blue to red, purple, lemon-yellow, hot-pink, and a lurid bright green that rang a small bell of recognition somewhere in my brain.

I replaced the bundle of pens, just as Morley returned carrying a tray, on which there were a teapot with strings from two bags hanging out, two mismatched cups and saucers, and a cream and sugar combo from two different sets. He put the tray down on the table and smiled, warily. I smiled back.

"Shall I be Mum?" I asked, picking up the teapot and pouring. We busied ourselves with sugar and milk, then sat down, Morley in his recliner and me on the two-seater.

"What I came to talk about, Morley," I began.

"I'm glad you came," Morley said quickly. "Like I said, I don't get many visitors. It's a change. Is the tea all right?"

He took a sip of his, slopping some of it in the saucer when he replaced his cup.

"Don't be nervous, Morley," I said. "I just wanted to ask you if anyone else came into the museum after I left. Ruth Fernie, maybe?"

"No one came in," he said, shifting uneasily in his chair.

"When did you leave?"

"After I finished mopping the floors."

"Not long after I left, then."

"I guess not."

"Well, when I got back from lunch, I found this."

I took the defaced clipping out of my purse and held it out to him. He looked away.

"I shouldn't have done it," he said.

I almost didn't hear him, because I had just remembered where I had seen that bright green ink before, the bright green and all the rest that had been used to write the threatening letters. I looked at Morley, wondering if I should confront him about it.

"Are you mad at me for scribbling on the picture?" Morley asked.

"No, I'm not mad, just confused. Why?"

Morley shrugged.

"I don't know. I just did."

"Do you want to talk about it?"

"She was my sweetheart, once," he said.

"Yes, we talked about that. You were engaged."

"I didn't tell the truth before, when I said I was sick after the war. I was sick in the head. I just ruined everything."

"The war hurt a lot of people, Morley. Not just physical injuries. It's nothing to be ashamed of."

"I wasn't brave. I was a coward over there and people died because it was my fault. I couldn't marry her. I wasn't good enough for her any more."

"Did she say that?"

"No. But I knew, and that's why we didn't get married."

"Maybe you should have told her. You don't know what she would have said. Things might have turned out very differently for you. That must make you sad."

"No, I'm not sad. Only when I think about that time. When she went away. When she left me and went to play baseball."

"So memories about her upset you," I said. "That's understandable. Is that why you scribbled on her picture?"

He nodded his head.

"But you knew I might guess it was you, didn't you?"

"I almost took it away, but I thought you needed it for your article."

"Or maybe some part of you wanted to be caught," I said, carefully. "Is there something else you'd like to tell me?"

"No, I just got mad, seeing that picture. It brought back bad memories. It was stupid, I guess."

"Yes, but you still did it," I probed, "and you brought attention to yourself."

Silence.

"Is there something else you'd like to tell me?" I asked, one more time, not wanting to push too hard.

"No, there isn't anything else."

"You know, Morley, I was just looking at your things here," I said. "You've got quite a collection of pens. Coloured pens."

"People throw them away," he said. "Good things they just throw away. I keep them. That's all. No crime in that."

"Mr. Timms, some of the women from the league, like my mother, like Virna Wilton, got letters before they came for the induction," I said, gently. "Letters telling them not to come. Letters written in all different colours of ink, like yours."

Morley drank his tea, looking miserable.

"Those letters," I continued, "said that women like my mum don't deserve to be in the Hall of Fame. Is that what you think?"

"She's not like the rest," he said. "She's a nice lady."

"Yes, she is," I said. "But those letters she got frightened her. Why do you think the person that sent the letters wanted to frighten a nice lady like her? Or Mrs. Deneka, the poor old soul. Why would he want to frighten her?"

"Maybe he just wanted to make them not come. And, see, it would have been better if they stayed away. If they did what the letters said, because look what went and happened."

We were getting into some uncharted territory. I should back off and call Andy. But I didn't want to lose the moment.

"Yes, Morley," I said. "Look what went and happened. Virna Wilton died."

"I didn't mean it to happen," Morley said. "I never meant it to happen. I swear it."

"Why don't you tell me about it," I said.

He hunched in his big chair, his hands clasped between his knees, looking like a guilty, frightened child, rocking slightly back and forth.

"Go ahead, Morley," I said. "You'll feel better when you talk about it."

"I didn't know what was going to happen, I swear it," he said. "I didn't want them to come is all. Like I said, it brings back memories, bad feelings. I thought if I scared them they would stay away, and then I wouldn't have to have the feelings."

"So you wrote the letters," I said.

"Yes. I'm sorry. It was wrong. Will I have to go to jail?"

"That depends, Morley. It depends on what else you have to tell me."

"That's all. That's all I have to tell."

He looked up, suddenly, with a new fear on his face.

"You mean you think I killed Virna myself?"

"Did you? Maybe not meaning to?"

He shook his head wildly.

"Did you see Virna Wilton that night? After the banquet was over? Did you talk to her?"

"No, I swear to God I didn't."

"I saw you in the bar that night. Virna was there, too."

"I was just there to keep Garth company. No harm."

"I believe you, Morley," I said, and I did. The poor old man was terrified. I put out my hand and patted his. He burst into tears.

CHAPTER

35

It took me about half an hour and several cups of tea to calm Morley down. In truth, confession had taken away a great load of stress from an old man not accustomed to it. I tried to reassure him that the Mounties were unlikely to put him in jail for writing the letters. By the time I left, he seemed to be his chirpy self again, to the point that he was offering to show me his extensive string collection. I took a pass, and headed across the river to North Battleford.

I took the old highway, the scenic route down the valley to the low bridge over the North Saskatchewan River, a sluggish, meandering stream the colour of mud. The bridge touched down on Finlayson Island halfway across, a park with walking trails that I wished I'd had time to explore, but I figured I better go talk to the police about Morley.

Once at the RCMP detachment, I had to state my business to a receptionist through a speaking vent in the presumably bullet-proof enquiries window. I asked for either Andy or Sergeant Deutsch, and gave my name. She punched up a number on her phone, spoke, and buzzed me in. Andy came out of an office door into the central office area, clearly surprised to see me.

"What are you doing here?" he asked.

"I have some news for you," I said. "Is this a bad time?"

"What sort of news? What have you done now?"

"Relax, it's nothing dangerous. I think Sergeant Deutsch should hear it too."

He sighed and took my arm, leading me into the GIS office, where Don Deutsch and Hugh Grenfell both sat, drinking coffee.

"Kate, this is a surprise," Deutsch said, pleasantly enough. He got me a chair. "Would you like a coffee?"

"No, I've just had tea. And I have some information that might be important."

"Try us."

"I found out who wrote the letters," I said. "It was Morley Timms. He told me he did."

"He told you," Andy said. "Just like that. What, you were hanging around, you and Morley, just shooting the shit and he said, by the way, I wrote those letters everybody's so worked up about?"

"Well, no. I kind of figured it out and asked him about it."

"Maybe you should back up a pace or two and explain how this happened," Deutsch said.

I went through the defaced clipping and going to ask Morley about it; seeing the pens and realizing that they were similar to the ones that had been used to write the letters. That's where Andy interrupted me.

"At which point it didn't occur to you to just get out of there and come talk to us?"

"I didn't want to lose the moment," I muttered.

Deutsch rubbed his hand across his eyes.

"Didn't want to lose the moment. Jesus wept."

"So Old Morley admitted he did that?" Grenfell asked.

"Yes. It wasn't hard to get him to admit to writing them. He wanted to talk about it."

"Did he say why?"

"He apparently has some sort of bad feelings about the league that have to do with his past with Wilma. He thought he could scare the Belles into staying away. It's kind of sad. He won't have to go to jail, will he?"

Deutsch looked at Andy.

"Like you said, she has an uncanny way of getting right in the middle of things."

"Look, I didn't know when I went there," I said, "but I was looking around his place while he made tea, and I saw all these different coloured pens he had, so . . ."

"So you decided to play detective," Deutsch said.

"Then, he was really stressed, so I told him he wouldn't have to go to jail."

"Oh, you played detective, judge, and jury, too," Andy said.

"I'm sorry, okay? He also said he didn't have anything to do with the murder. I believed him."

"No, I can't see Morley for the murder, either," Deutsch said. "But we'd better talk to the silly old bugger anyway. Give him a call, Hughie. Tell him we're coming over."

Grenfell picked up the phone.

"Did Morley have anything else to say?" Deutsch asked.

"He rambled on a bit about his war experiences, and how he wasn't good enough to marry Wilma. Later, he changed the story, said that the league had ruined his life. That if it hadn't been for baseball, Wilma would have stayed with him, waiting for him to get well."

"She'd still be waiting, then," Deutsch snorted.

Grenfell hung up the phone.

"Busy," he said.

"I'll drop in on him on the way home," Deutsch said, then turned back to us. "This takes care of one loose end, anyway. We don't have to find a way to tie the letters to Rowley."

"Oh, that reminds me, Mrs. Fernie came by the Hall of Fame just before lunch. She says her nephew couldn't have done it."

"Duh," Grenfell said. "What did you expect? She'll defend him because he's family."

"She seemed pretty convinced."

"Thanks for passing along the message," Deutsch said. "As a matter of fact, I'm beginning to have my doubts about him. He and his lawyer were awfully cooperative this morning. They agreed to supply hair and blood samples, and to a search of his house."

"I'm not ready to write Morley Timms off," Andy said. "There's clearly bitterness there, and it's had a long time to fester. Seeing Virna in that uniform could have triggered some sort of flashback."

"But he has no history of violence, none at all," Deutsch said. "The guy's the town eccentric. Strange, yes. Dangerous, no. His only record dates way back to just after the war, when there were some drunken disturbances, but since then, nothing. We look after our own here, and Morley's a solid citizen. Peculiar, but solid. Everyone loves old Morley."

"Tell them about the hat," Grenfell said, chuckling.

"Yeah, this is typical Morley. He gets a disability pension from the government, but he does general odd jobs around town, too. Some carpentry, repairs, caretaking here and there, like at the Hall of Fame, things like that. Like I say, we look after our own. But every once in a while, he up and decides it's time for a holiday. There's never any warning, no rhyme or reason to it. But what he does, see, when he decides to take time off, he has this checked cap, a red checked cap, an old hunting cap with earflaps, that he wears. And if you see Morley around town in that damned checked cap, winter or summer, you know he's on holiday and isn't going to show up at work."

"How long do these vacations last?" I asked.

"Sometimes a day, sometimes a week, sometimes more, sometimes less," Deutsch said.

"When he's got the hat on, it's like he's invisible," Grenfell said. "Then one day, boom, he puts another hat on and he's back on the job. He's quite a character. But, like Don said, he's harmless."

"You can come with me when I talk to him, if you like, Andy," Deutsch said.

"No, you know the guy. I trust your instincts. I'm going to go back to the hotel and maybe talk to Jack Wilton a little more."

"We'll all keep digging," Deutsch said. "I'll talk to you later. After I see Morley."

Andy and I drove back in our separate cars. I was grateful for the solitude. I was in no mood for another scene about Jack Wilton.

CHAPTER

36

I ran into the Denekas when I got back to the hotel. They were coming out of their room, near the elevator on Andy's and my floor. He was struggling with two suitcases. She looked awful.

"Is everything all right?" I asked.

"Meg's had one of her spells," he said. She looked at me with empty eyes. "We're going home now. Her doctor is waiting."

I took one of the bags.

"Let me help you."

"Thanks."

We rode down in silence, except for a strange humming sound from Meg.

Andy was in the lobby. He assessed the situation instantly and took both the Denekas' bags and led them out the door. Peter Deneka turned to me on his way out.

"Say goodbye to everybody. Your parents and Edna. Thank them for me, and tell them I'm sorry."

He led his wife out into the rain, one of the saddest sights I've ever seen.

When we got upstairs, Andy claimed the first shower. I called home to check on Elwy. I could tell from Sally's voice that the news wasn't good.

"I just talked to the vet," she said.

"And?"

"And it looks bad, Kate."

"How bad?"

"The worst," she said. "It's his heart. She said it's, wait a sec, I've got it written down. Cardiomyopathy. That means blood clots in his heart. And kidney failure, Dr. Reeve says."

"But he was fine before, you said."

I was grasping at a very weak straw, and I knew it. Andy, who had just come out of the shower, stopped towelling his hair and looked at me, concerned.

"Isn't there anything else she can do?" I asked. "More tests? Some kind of treatment?"

"He's not going to get better, Kate. I'm sorry."

"Oh, shit. Talk to Andy," I said, and held out the phone. He took it and asked Sally a couple of questions. Then he told her to hold on and turned to me.

"Sally says that she and T.C. will go and be with him," he said. "Or the vet will wait until you get home."

"I don't know what to do," I said. "I should be there with him."

I looked out the window at the parking lot. Andy put his arm around me, and rubbed my back.

"Just a second, Sally," he said into the phone, then put the receiver to his chest.

"It's up to you, Kate," he said, softly, "but I think you should just let him go. Sally says he's in pain now."

"But he'll feel like I've betrayed him," I said.

"No, *you'll* feel like you betrayed him. I think he'll be happy just to go to sleep."

"I don't want him to suffer," I said.

"Sally agrees," he said. "She says that T.C. says so, too. He said to tell you he'll hold Elwy while he gets the shot."

"Oh, God, that's so brave of him," I said, tearing up.

"Elwy will feel safe with him. You know that."

"Tell her," I took a deep breath, "tell her to go ahead."

"Do you want to tell her yourself?"

I shook my head and curled up on the bed.

"When is this going to happen?" Andy asked into the phone. "I see. All right. I'll tell her. Thanks."

"Wait, don't hang up," I said. He told Sally to hold on.

"Do you think . . . " I was embarrassed. "Do you think we could get his ashes? I'll put them in the garden."

I broke down again. Andy relayed my question, then hung up.

"Sally's going to take care of it," he said. "She'll save the ashes and you can all do it together."

"All the flowers will grow big and fat," I said, trying to smile. "He was useless all his life. I might as well put him to work now."

Andy lay down next to me and wrapped me in his arms.

"I just want to go home."

"Let's go."

"Don't you have to stay?"

"They don't need me any more," he said. "They can handle the rest of the investigation. I was only really needed that first day when there were so many people to talk to. We can go tomorrow, if you like."

That decided, Andy went to the ice machine so we could have a drink. I called my parents and arranged to meet them in the hotel restaurant. As a special concession, they agreed to wait until six to eat.

"Did you tell them about Elwy?" Andy asked.

"They were very sympathetic," I said. "They never said he was only a cat."

He handed me a drink.

"To Elwy," he said, raising his glass. "He was a fine and noble cat."

"To fine and noble Elwy who had a good long life."

"And to leaving the lovely Battlefords," he alliterated.

"At long last," I agreed.

"Do I sense disenchantment with small-town prairie life?"

"From me? No. Except I have been having erotic dreams about grilled octopus on the Danforth."

"And retsina, and a small Greek coffee after."

"And walking down the street at midnight and still seeing people awake."

"And traffic that doesn't stop for pedestrians."

"And traffic, period."

"And our own bed."

"I'll drink to that," I said.

The phone rang. It was Don Deutsch. Andy took the phone from me, listened for a few moments, swore, then hung up.

"What is it?"

"Morley Timms has shot himself. Don's picking me up."

"Suicide? Morley? Oh, no."

"So it seems. He left a note, apparently. Addressed to you."

"A note to me? Why?"

"I don't know. Don didn't say."

Andy grabbed his jacket and headed for the door.

"Wait," I said. "I'm coming with you."

"No way."

"The note is for me, I have a right to go."

"Kate, the man shot himself in the head. Think about it. This is not a crime scene you want to see."

That gave me pause.

"I'll call as soon as I know anything," he said.

I took a shower, then went to my parents' room and told them what had happened.

"Andy was wise to have you stay here," my mother said.

"I just hate to be shut out of things," I said. "I hate it when he treats me like an outsider."

"But you are, Kate," my mother said. "Police officers have to see and do a lot of unpleasant and dangerous things. Andy is just trying to protect you."

"I don't need protection," I said, sounding petulant and stupid even to my own ears.

"We'll go have supper, and wait for Andy to come back," my father said. "He can tell us all about it."

We went down to the restaurant. We had just sat down when Jack and Edna appeared, so we asked them to join us.

"I was looking for you, Reverend Henry," Jack said. "I have a favour to ask."

"I hope I can grant it," he said.

"Well, the police are releasing my mother's, her remains, tomorrow. I have decided to have her cremated here. That's what she wanted, cremation, so her ashes could be put with Aunt Wilma's. At the old ballpark. That's where they both wanted to be. Anyway, I've spoken to a funeral home, and they will take care of all the details. And, well, frankly, it's a lot easier to transport ashes."

"A sensible decision," my father said.

"My mother wasn't a church-going woman," Jack explained, apologetically, "but her roots were in your church. I'd like you to say a few words at the funeral home. Not really a service. More like a, well, a blessing."

"I could arrange a service, if you like," Daddy said. "I'm sure the local man would be glad to let us use the church."

Jack shook his head.

"Under the circumstances, I'd be happier with something more low-key. I thought we could just have people who knew her gather together to see her on her way. And then I'd drive Edna back to Watrous and take Mother home."

"Whatever you like," my father said. "I would be honoured."

"I'm sure that some of the people from the Hall of Fame would like to come, too," Edna said. "And we should invite Garth Elshaw and Morley Timms."

Oh, dear. My parents looked at me, and I told Jack and Edna about Morley's death.

"What, I mean, when? Why?" Jack asked.

242

"I'm not sure. I was there earlier this afternoon, and it happened since then. Andy's there with the police now."

"Morley wrote the threatening letters," my father said. "That's what Kate found out. Perhaps he regretted the pain he caused."

"There's another reason to kill himself," Jack said. "Because he killed my mother."

"He denied it when I talked to him," I said. "I believed him, then. Now I don't know what to think. He left a note, addressed to me, Andy said. Not that they've let me read it. Anyway, that might be some kind of explanation."

"What did he tell you about the letters?" Jack asked.

"It all went back to his relationship with Wilma, somehow. He said he didn't want to relive bad memories. He didn't exactly make sense. I should never have left him alone."

"Don't, Kate," my father said. "You couldn't have known."

"But I was the one that confronted him and made him admit to writing the letters. That obviously sent him over the edge."

"You can't blame yourself," he said. "As you said yourself, he seemed fine when you left."

"Well, he obviously wasn't, was he?"

"Did he blame poor Virna for his breakup with Wilma?" my mother asked.

"He was all over the map about that. He said at one point that he understood why they could never marry, he and Wilma, because of the way he was after the war, but later he seemed to blame baseball for taking her away."

"Well, I'm not sure I understand anything any more," Edna said. "What about the other man? Does this mean he didn't do it?"

"We'll have to wait to hear from the police," I said. "Andy said he would let us know as soon as he found out what was up."

The waitress came to take our orders. When we were done, the subject of Morley's death was dropped until Andy's return. We talked about Elwy instead, which didn't do much to cheer me up. After dinner, I left them with their coffee and went up to the room to wait for Andy's call.

CHAPTER

37

When the knock came at the door ten minutes later, I was surprised to find my mother standing in the hall. She looked nervous, uncertain, not like herself at all.

"Hi, Mum," I said. "Where's Daddy?"

"He and Jack Wilton are discussing the plans for the service tomorrow."

"Do you want to come in?"

She walked into the room with a strange, tense, determination. I realized that it was the first time we had been alone together on the whole trip.

"I have something to tell you," she said.

She sat down in one of the armchairs and took a deep breath.

"Can I get you anything?" I asked. "A glass of water? You don't look well."

"I believe I would like to have a small bit of that whisky," she said, astonishing me.

I poured it, and one for myself, with some of the ice from Andy's pre-dinner bucket. My mother took a small sip, then began to speak.

"What I am about to say is not going to be easy for either one of us," she said. "It may cause you some pain. I ask that you try not to judge me too harshly. I think it may help to explain a number of things. And I ask also for your discretion."

"Are you all right, Mum?"

"No, I'm not. But I have to do this. I know you well enough to realize that you will find it out anyway, but I want you to hear it from me. Please don't make it more difficult."

My mother sat very straight, holding onto her glass with both hands, her eyes fixed on a point somewhere in the centre of the room. I lit a cigarette.

"I know you've always resented my strictness," she said. "We have had enough arguments over the years about your behaviour to know that."

"Mum, you don't have to . . ."

"Please." She held her hand up, palm out. "Let me say my piece. I was strict, yes, but the only reason I acted that way was so you could avoid the pain I have suffered."

Another tiny sip of Scotch, and a visible pulling together of her determination.

"When I was young, I made a mistake. It's a mistake I have lived with every day of my life since then. When I was playing baseball, I met a young man and fell in love with him. He was an American. His name was Carl Johannsen."

"Mrs. Deneka mentioned him to me," I said.

"Yes, she was confused."

"What happened to this man, this Carl?"

"He died in France, during the war. At Normandy."

"I'm sorry."

"You shouldn't be," she said, with a small, tight, smile. "If he hadn't died, you would never have been born. I was going to marry him, you see, after he came back home. I would never have met your father."

She paused, then looked at me, imploringly.

"Things were different in wartime," she said. "People did things they never would have, otherwise."

She looked away again, back to middle distance.

"In my case, before Carl left, I gave myself to him. He was the first man I had ever been with. I loved him very much, and he wanted, we both wanted, to seal our pact, our promise to each other."

I wasn't sure which of us was the most uncomfortable. I began to suspect where this was leading.

"He had never been with a woman either. It was the first time for both of us. It happened during spring training before he went overseas. As it turned out, it was the last time. And also, as it turned out, I got pregnant. Ironic, isn't it?"

She laughed. It was heartbreaking.

"I found out just after the start of the 1944 season. In those days there was a terrible stigma attached to unmarried pregnancy. I felt ashamed, and I didn't know who to turn to. I couldn't tell my family. I couldn't, I wouldn't, have an abortion. I didn't know what to do. Finally, I told Virna, who was my best friend on the team. She figured it all out."

"Jack," I said.

"He is my son. Mine and Carl Johannsen's."

The room seemed to tilt, suddenly. I wanted to reach out to her, but didn't know how. I couldn't even find words to speak.

She wiped tears from her eyes, then took a deep breath.

"The details probably don't matter, but this is how it happened," she said, her voice without expression. "Virna took charge, the way she always did. The first thing she did was announce her marriage. Of course, she made the husband up. She used the name of a cousin of hers, who really was in the army, overseas. Then she began a correspondence with him. When his letters arrived, she pretended they were from her husband."

"But what about you? Did no one realize you were pregnant?"

"No, I never carried any of my children big. And the baby wasn't born until late November. November 27th. 1944."

She took a deep breath, fighting for control.

"I was in good shape, remember, from playing baseball. I got teased about getting fat, but that was all."

"What about Virna? Did she say she was pregnant?"

"No. The next spring she showed up with the baby and told them she had played pregnant and didn't want the league to know."

I wanted her to stop, just stop talking, but she wouldn't. She couldn't until she was done.

"I didn't go home after the season, of course. I told my parents that I had a job in the States for the winter, which made them very unhappy. Virna and I went to Chicago and rented a room. I had the child, using Virna's name, and the name of her cousin as the father."

"She knew she couldn't have children," I said.

My mother nodded.

"She knew, but she wanted one desperately. This way, we could both go on. She was willing to raise the child on her own. I was never brave enough for that."

We sat in silence for a few moments.

"Now you understand why I didn't want you digging into the past. Why I wanted the secret to go with Virna to her grave. But you wouldn't let go of it. You always were a stubborn child."

She smiled weakly. I waited to see if she had anything more to say, but she just sat, looking into the glass she still held in both hands.

"Daddy doesn't know, I take it," I said, finally.

She shook her head.

"Are you going to tell him? And Jack? Will you tell him?"

"It's best to leave well enough alone. Jack is Virna's son. He always has been."

"But now he has no family. You could give him that."

"I've thought of that. But I don't know if I am willing to hurt your father to do it."

"It's your decision," I said. "Whatever you decide, I'll support you."

"I don't think I made a mistake giving him to Virna," she said, almost to herself. "She did a good job with him, didn't she?"

"Yes, he's a nice man. Does he look like his father?"

"Exactly," she said, with a slight shudder. "He's older than Carl was when I knew him, of course. Carl was just a boy when he died, really. But I see it in his eyes and his chin. The set of his mouth. Just like Carl."

"He was a very handsome man, then," I said, inanely. I wanted her to go, just go away.

She put down her glass and stood up.

"I'd better be getting back to your father," she said. "He'll be wondering."

All I could do was watch as she crossed the room to the bathroom. I lit another cigarette, my hands trembling. I could hear the water running. When she came back into the room, her tears were gone. She was back in control.

"Will you keep the secret?" she asked, briskly.

"It's not mine to share."

"Thank you."

She opened the door.

"Don't think too badly of me," she said, not turning around. Then she was gone, and I was the one in tears.

CHAPTER

38

I cried until I couldn't any more, until all the emotion of the day had drained away. I cried for my mother and for Morley and for Elwy, tears of sadness, anger, and confusion.

How had she lived with this all these years, raising her daughters, knowing that she had a son growing up too? Virna wrote letters to her from time to time. They must have included news about Jack. Had she sent photos, too? My poor mother, carrying this secret, and her own shame, for more than fifty years.

My father is a forgiving man, but I understood why she hadn't shared the burden with him. She wouldn't want to hurt him. It would undermine everything they had built together.

And I wished that she had never shared her secret with me.

Finally, like my mother, I went and washed my face with cold water and sucked in all the pain. When Andy came back, I was in control again. He called from the lobby.

"Are you okay?" he asked.

"Never better."

"Yeah, sure. Are you up to meeting us in Jack Wilton's room? I think you should be there. It's 428. We're in the lobby, on our way there now."

"Why?"

"I guess to let him know who killed his mother."

"Morley?"

"He confessed in the note."

"Oh, shit."

"Room 428."

"I'll be there."

I took the stairs up a flight, and got there at the same time as the elevator delivered Andy and Donald Deutsch. Jack's door was open. He was inside, clearing piles of clothes off various surfaces, making room for us to sit down.

"Sorry about the mess," he said. I found myself unable to look at him.

Deutsch sat in one chair, I sat in the other, Jack was on the edge of the bed, and Andy leaned against the desk, arms crossed.

"We've brought copies of the letter that Morley Timms wrote before he shot himself," Deutsch said. "It indicates that he suicided out of remorse for killing your mother."

He handed one to me and one to Jack.

"Just have a read, and we'll answer any questions you might have afterwards."

I looked at the note, which was written in the same cramped hand as the warning letters.

To: Miss Kate Henry

I'm glad you made me tell the truth. Honesty is the Best Policy. That is why I am writing this letter. I'm sorry for everything I did. Please tell your Mother and the other ladies. I shouldn't have done it.

Wilma Elshaw was the LOVE OF MY LIFE until she was STOLEN AWAY by that unnatural woman, that ABOMINATION whose name I will not write down. It was the girls baseball and the LOW MORAL CLIMATE that turned my beloved Wilma from me. When I saw that Old Woman prancing around in her baseball dress like a harlot, it got my goat. She is in the Hall of Fame like she wanted, but her soul is ROASTING IN HELL.

But I shouldn't have tried to frighten the other ladies. That was wrong.

Yours sincerely,
Morley Timms.

I finished reading it, and looked at Jack.

"There's a lot of hatred in this letter," he said, his voice slightly unsteady. "He sure hid it well."

"He did," Deutsch said. "He hid it for all these years."

"What an unhappy life he must have had," I said.

"I imagine the rage was buried pretty deep," Andy said. "It took seeing Virna to trigger it off."

"Who found Morley?" I asked.

"Garth Elshaw," Deutsch said. "Morley had phoned him, he said. He was evidently very agitated, so Garth went to his house to settle him down. When he knocked, Morley didn't answer. The door was locked. Garth kept knocking, then heard a shot. He broke down the door. A neighbour heard the commotion and called 911."

"Did he do it with the shotgun I saw?"

"No, an old revolver," Deutsch said. "Probably a wartime souvenir. He's lucky it still worked. If lucky's the right word."

Jack closed his eyes and took a deep, steadying breath.

"So it's over."

"There are still a few things to clear up," Don said. "There will be an autopsy, and we'll send samples to the lab for comparisons, but, yes, it's over."

He stood up, and the rest of us followed suit. Deutsch shook Jack's hand and offered his condolences again.

"I hope you'll come to the service for my mother tomorrow."

"Of course."

Then Andy shook his hand and we went into the hall.

"I don't know about you, but I could use a drink," Deutsch said. "Want to join me?"

"Kate, what do you want to do?" Andy asked.

"You go ahead. I should go tell my parents."

"You deserve it," Don said. "You were the one who figured it out."

"I was the one that got the guy dead."

"You saved the people of Canada some money. That's worth drinking to."

"I'll see, after I tell my parents. By the way, has anyone told Ruth Fernie's nephew he's off the hook?"

"Hugh Grenfell's over there right now. He hasn't got anything to worry about."

They headed down the stairs and I went and knocked on my parents' door. My mother answered. We had a hard time meeting each other's eyes. I told them what had happened.

"I just wish I knew why," I said.

"We'll never know, now," Daddy said.

I said good night to them and went and found Andy and Don at a table in a relatively quiet corner. I was sick of the bar, with its cracked Formica tables, annoying gambling machines and non-stop rock and country videos. I was also sick of the clientele, a depressing bunch of characters. I lit up what was probably my tenth cigarette since my mother's visit. So much for cutting back.

After our drinks came, I brought up Morley Timms.

"Do you think he would have been convicted?" I asked.

"He would have ended up locked up somewhere," Don said. "Either maximum security psychiatric or in the jug."

"The poor man's better off dead," I said.

"Probably," Andy agreed. "I wonder if he meant to kill Virna. Would you have gone for first degree on this one, Don?"

"Depends on his statement, depends on the crown attorney. You know how these things go. A man Morley's age, it isn't going to matter whether it's first degree, second degree, or manslaughter, because he's going to die in jail however it turns out."

"Do you ever feel badly about putting someone in jail?" I asked. "Someone like Morley, who was kind of pathetic and unlikely to ever do it again?"

"You do the crime, you got to do the time," Don shrugged.

"Everything is so cut and dried with you guys," I said. "Everything that isn't white is black."

"No, I see greys, too," Don said. "I also see all the pretty colours. But my job is to uphold the law."

"It's no use, Don," Andy said. "She's a stubborn one."

"Only when I'm right," I said.

"Which you always are," Andy answered.

I wasn't in the mood to play. I butted my cigarette and drained my drink.

"No hard feelings, but it's been a tough day. I'm for bed."

I packed my cigarettes into my purse and stood up.

"And even though we disagree, as a sign of conciliation, I will allow you law-abiding chaps to pay for my drink."

"Glad to do it," Don said. "I've enjoyed sparring with you."

"Maybe we'll go a few rounds another time when I'm not so tired," I said.

"I won't be long," Andy said.

"No rush. I'll be asleep anyway."

Which I was, the moment my head hit the pillow.

CHAPTER

39

The funeral was at two the next afternoon. The gathering was small and the ceremony was brief but comforting. My father spoke with quiet eloquence about loss, grieving, and forgiveness. Jack spoke, movingly, about his mother and her importance in his life. I didn't dare look in my mother's direction, but knew the pain she must be feeling. It was all over in fifteen minutes, and we were back in the parking lot in the sunshine. In addition to my parents, Jack, Edna, Andy, and me, there were a few locals. Don Deutsch, Hugh Grenfell, and Walt Digby came from the RCMP; Dave Shury from the Hall of Fame was there with his wife, Jane; Garth Elshaw, who must have been still reeling from the shock of his friend's death; and, surprisingly, Ruth Fernie.

I wanted to talk to Garth, who stood a bit apart, waiting to have a word with Jack, but I didn't know what to say. Andy interrupted my indecision before I could make my move.

"Do you mind going back alone?" he asked. "I'm going for a coffee with Walt Digby. He'll drop me back at the hotel."

"That's fine. Don't be too long. I'll finish packing and check out."

Garth was in conversation with Jack by then, so I felt somewhat let off the hook. I told my parents I would see them back at the hotel and hopped in the Grapemobile, something else I was going to be glad to see the last of.

I took the old highway back towards Battleford, pulling off the road when I got to Finlayson Island. I was a little overdressed for hiking, but I was wearing flat shoes, which would be fine for easy walking. I had half an hour to kill.

The parking lot was empty, which was a surprise on such a beautiful afternoon. I walked down the trail through the trees until I came to the river's edge. I could hear birds singing, but, as usual, couldn't find them without help from Andy. He's the bird-watcher. The only time I'm any good at finding the damn things is in the spring and fall, when there aren't any leaves.

I found a log by the path near the shore to sit on, and watched some ducks swimming, a mother and four babies. It was good to be alone.

Aside from the faint sound of cars on the bridge and the birds, it was quiet. I closed my eyes and held my face to the afternoon sun and breathed in the peace.

Then I heard something, an animal, maybe, crackling through the brush. I sat up and saw Garth Elshaw come down the trail.

"Mr. Elshaw! You startled me," I said.

258

"I saw that purple car from the road. I thought I would find you and that Munro fellow."

"Well, Andy's not here. He's with the RCMP officers."

"I guess you'll be heading back east now."

"Yes, tomorrow," I said. "We're flying out of Saskatoon. We might even drive down tonight, depending on how my parents feel. I'm glad you found me. I was going to say goodbye after the funeral, but I didn't want to interrupt your talk with Jack."

"Well, I wanted to tell him I had no hard feelings. He said he might come up for a visit sometime."

"I'm glad," I said.

"I guess I'm the closest thing to family he's got, now."

Little did he know.

"I guess you are," I said.

"What are you doing walking around here?"

"It was a nice day. I like to get away from people sometimes. Sometimes I prefer the birds for company."

"There's a great horned owl down the path," he said, not taking the hint. "She sleeps in the same tree a lot. You ever seen one of those?"

"We have them back east, too."

"I'm not much of one for birds. Morley liked them. He liked to walk around here. That's why I came by this way. Thinking about him and all."

Garth looked slightly embarrassed by this display of sentiment. I kicked myself for trying to brush him off.

"Of course," I said. "You were friends for a long time."

"Over seventy years."

"Shall we walk for a while?" I asked.

"I recall him telling me about some birds he saw last week, some avocets, he said."

"I don't think I've ever seen one of those," I said.

"They have long legs, and this curious kind of bill. Sort of pretty, and comical at the same time. Called the American avocet. At the far point of the island, he said. I thought I'd go have a look at them."

"Do you mind if I come along?"

"Suit yourself."

We walked down the trail, side by side when it was wide enough. He led the way when it got narrow. We followed the path away from the shore, into the woods.

"I'm sorry about your friend," I said. "I can't help wondering if what we talked about upset him and made him, you know, do what he did. But when I left him, he seemed fine. He really did. I just wish I had stayed."

"I don't know how he could have been fine," Elshaw said. "When he called me on the phone, he was raving, he was as crazy as I've ever heard him."

"What did he say?"

"How the police were after him, they were coming to get him, I had to help him get away. He said he couldn't go to jail. He was afraid of prison. He was afraid of being locked up again."

"But I told him he wasn't going to have to go to jail."

"Well, he didn't believe you."

"I'm just so sorry. I'd give anything to have prevented it."

Elshaw touched my arm and pointed at a tree just off the path.

"Look there, now. There's the owl."

Following his finger I could make out the distinctive shape with its tufted ears.

"Saw one go after a cat one time," Elshaw said. "Almost got him, too."

Not a pleasant thought. We continued down the path.

"Mr. Elshaw, did it surprise you, about Morley, I mean?"

"Now that I look back, he was saying some strange things before the banquet. But I didn't think anything about it."

"What kind of strange things?" I asked.

"About the time after the war when Wilma left to play baseball. You know, instead of sticking with him. He got kind of worked up about it. His memory twisted things sometimes. I guess he believed it was her fault, Virna's."

"Did he talk about her over the years?"

"No. Just since this Hall of Fame thing came up. He hadn't even seen her since way back then."

"Even when she came and visited?"

"He stayed away then. She didn't want to see him, neither."

"He said he came as your guest to the banquet. Why did he come, if he was so bitter about the past?"

"He goes to all the dinners, seeing as how he works there and all. I thought he should be there. I thought it was the right thing. If he saw all those women as old ladies, he'd see there was nothing to get mad at."

"He certainly seemed to be having a good time that night," I said. "We were sitting together."

We were just coming out of the woods and heading down a little hill on slippery mud from the previous day's rain. The smooth leather soles of my shoes didn't give me any traction, and my left foot slid out from under me. I would have fallen, if Garth hadn't turned and grabbed my arm.

"Careful now," he said. "You don't want to fall."

"Thank you. These aren't the best shoes for walking."

"It's not much further now," he said, and started off again.

"Mr. Elshaw, what do you think happened that night? I mean, I saw you both at the bar afterwards, along with all those women. Did you leave before Morley?"

"We left at the same time. Morley drove that night. He doesn't drink. He let me off, and that's all I know."

"What time was that? I didn't see you leave."

"We just had one drink. Morley had ginger ale. Probably 12:15. No later."

"Then what?"

"What do you mean?"

"I mean do you figure he went back to the hotel? Or did he find her in the Hall of Fame?"

"What did he tell you?"

"He didn't tell me anything, except that he didn't have anything to do with it. I'm just trying to figure out how it happened. Because it's so hard to believe he did it."

"I guess he must have went back to the hotel."

"But why? How did he know what room she was in? She was last seen going to her room. Alone."

"Beats me. But that's what he must have done. Maybe he wanted to talk to her."

"Edna told me that Virna wanted to go and play a practical joke on her team-mates, but didn't know how to get in. If she ran into him after she left, maybe she asked him to take her there. Do you think?"

262

Elshaw behind me, now, on the narrow path, didn't answer.

"Then when they got there, how do you think it happened?"

"Maybe she said something that made him mad and he just took the bat and hit her. He probably didn't mean to kill her. It was, like they say, involuntary. Because Morley never would hurt a fly. After he hit her, he panicked, and took his tie and finished her off. He didn't want to get in trouble. Maybe he wasn't thinking too clearly. Got confused, likely."

"But why? What had she ever done to him?"

"She stole Wilma away from him. Into a life of shame. That's how he saw it."

The path had come close to the river again. I could see it through the bushes, a wet silty beach littered with driftwood logs. Elshaw stopped.

"You want to see them avocets," he said, "Morley said they were by this point, just here. Let me look."

He moved past me and leaned out over the water, holding onto the trunk of a black birch, looking to his right.

"Yes, they're there. Take a look. Be quiet, though. You don't want to scare them away."

He stepped back and I took his place. There was a weedy cove and there, wading in the shallow water among some reeds, were the avocets. As he had said, very comical birds, about eighteen inches tall, with upward curving bills and rusty heads. They were wonderful, dipping those splendid bills in the water, swishing them back and forth. I watched them for a few minutes, but my mind was on something Elshaw had said. Something that didn't seem right.

"Mr. Elshaw," I said, my eyes still on the birds. "When did Morley tell you all of this?"

"He didn't. He never said anything. I was just guessing."

"Then how did you know about him hitting her with the bat? How did you know about the necktie?"

"I read about it in the paper, I guess."

"But none of those details were in the paper," I said. "The police were keeping that confidential."

I turned to look at him. It was as if a stranger had taken Elshaw's place. His thick glasses couldn't hide the cold rage in his eyes that transformed him from a bland old man to someone much more dangerous. Next thing I knew, I was in very cold water, and he was right behind me. It became very quickly obvious that helping me wasn't what he had in mind.

40

"What are you doing?" I shouted, but I knew the answer. He was trying to push my head under water. Luckily, it was shallow enough for me to be able to twist around and brace myself on my knees in the clinging mud, making his job difficult.

"Shut up," he said. "You know too much."

"I don't know what you're talking about. Let me up."

I struggled, but he was strong for an old man. He stood in the knee-deep water and grabbed me around the waist from behind, one hand on my breast, mashing it painfully.

"You should have left well enough alone. Now I have to kill you, too."

I started to yell. He planted a big palm over my mouth.

"Here's the deal," he said, panting slightly. "You were walking along the path here, see. Then you slipped in your fancy shoes. Then you hit your head on a log here. Then you drowned."

I tried to speak, but he kept his hand over my mouth. Half my nose was blocked as well. I was having trouble breathing.

"I mean it," he said. "If I can kill my best friend, I can kill you easy."

I looked wildly around, trying to see if there was anyone whose attention I could attract, but we were out of view of the bridge, isolated on the little cove. I stopped struggling, trying to keep calm and think of what to do.

"Don't yell, now," he said. I shook my head. "I'm going to take my hand off your mouth. Are you going to yell?"

I shook my head once more, and he let me breathe. I gasped and coughed. He still had one arm wrapped around me.

"Why?" I asked, when I could.

"That woman put me through fifty years of shame. She dragged my sister into filth and ruined the family name. The shame killed my mother. And she just laughed at me."

"But why now? Why after all these years?"

He let out a harsh sound, a kind of sardonic bark.

"Because I could. I could get away with it. I almost did it thirty-five years ago. In the woods during hunting season. But the boy came along. I didn't want to hurt the boy. Now don't you move."

He climbed out of the water and stood on the bank, panting, but blocking my way out of the water. I could see by the expression on his face that I wouldn't be able to get past him.

"I would have got away with it clean, except for that old fool Morley telling you about the letters."

"All he told me was that he wrote them," I said, stalling for time.

"He wrote them to warn them away from me. That's what he told me when he called after he talked to you yesterday. He wasn't in any state. I made that up. He told me he knew I did it. He figured it all out. He threatened me."

"But he didn't say anything to me," I said. "I didn't know anything. You didn't have to do this. This was all unnecessary, don't you see?"

Also irrelevant. If I didn't know too much before, I did now. I kept talking to give my mind time to catch up.

"Look, Garth, don't make things worse for yourself," I said. "The police think Morley did it, the case is closed. Let me go and I'll just leave the Battlefords and never come back."

I wouldn't have bought it either. I looked at Elshaw, who was standing with his boots in the water. He was leaning towards where I was kneeling in the water, ready to make his move.

I made sure that my feet were braced under me in the mud, then slumped my shoulders and hung my head to look vulnerable, making sure I could still see his legs and feet. When he shifted them to move towards me, I straightened up as forcefully as I could, and butted him in the stomach.

He had to grab hold of a bush to keep from falling, and I was able to get to my feet, which put us on equal, if precarious, footing. When he grabbed me again, instead of pulling away, I pushed, setting him off-balance long enough to brace myself and drive my right knee up into his groin.

He shouted in pain, but kept his grip on my arms. We went at it half in and half out of the water.

By the time I managed to free my right arm, I was on the narrow beach, bent back painfully over a driftwood log, with the stub of a branch stabbing into my shoulder. His hands went around my throat. I could hear his rasping breath.

With my last strength, I pushed up and wrenched around to grab the log and flail it at his head. It connected and he went limp, pinning me into the muck. I rolled him off me and got up.

He lay on his back, with his eyes rolled up into their sockets. His glasses hung off his left ear and he was covered in mud and blood.

"Oh, shit," I said, and began to run as fast as I could back up the trail to the parking lot.

By the time I got there, I was wiped out. I'd lost my purse somewhere on the trail, with my car keys in it. I staggered up the last hill to the highway.

The first three cars swerved to avoid me and accelerated. I was wet, barefoot, covered in mud, and my hair was wild, sticking out in all directions. I probably looked like an escaped lunatic.

The fourth vehicle stopped, an old beat-up pickup driven by a tough-looking Indian with pock marks on his face. There was a gang of scraggy-looking teenagers riding in the back, but their baseball gear reassured me.

"You got problems, lady?" he asked.

"I've got to get to the police," I said. "There's a man hurt back there in the woods."

"Get in," he said. "Joe, you go get in back, make room for the lady."

One of the two teens did what he was told, and I squeezed in next to the other one.

"You don't look so hot yourself," the driver said.

"It's a long story."

"Who's the guy hurt?"

"That's a long story, too."

"Looks like you been in a fight," said the teen in the middle.

I closed my eyes and took a deep breath. The adrenalin had left my body in a rush, and I was shaking.

"Mud wrestling, maybe," he said, and snickered.

"You all right?" asked the driver.

"Yeah, I'm fine," I said, not opening my eyes.

"Well, we're here," he said. "RCMP headquarters."

I thanked him and got out of the truck.

"I'm sorry about the mud," I said. The whole bunch of them watched me walk up the front steps on rubbery legs. I got inside the door. The receptionist took one look at me and buzzed the door. I walked right through the bullpen, my shoes squelching with every step, and into the GIS office.

Don Deutsch looked up from his desk, then hung up the phone.

"What the hell?"

"I think I just killed Garth Elshaw," I said. Then I fell into a chair and burst into tears.

269

CHAPTER

41

Andy caught up with us by the river. I had told Deutsch, Hugh Grenfell, and some of the constables where I had last seen Garth Elshaw on the trail. He was still there. Not dead, as I had feared, but not very well either. He put up no resistance when they strapped him onto a stretcher.

"Damn it," Don Deutsch said as we watched the paramedics carry him out.

He was angry, and I didn't blame him. Morley Timms, a harmless old man, had died because the cops were busy chasing the wrong rainbows. Not to mention me, a harmless middle-aged woman, scared half to death.

"I've got to tell you, Andy Munro is right," Hugh Grenfell said. "Trouble just seems to find you."

"But this time I wasn't even looking for it. I was just taking a walk in the woods."

Three cars rolled into the parking lot. Leading the parade was a police cruiser, followed by my father's car and Jack Wilton's. The doors all popped open at once like some circus act, and the whole damn gang rolled out: my parents, Andy, Edna, and Jack. Andy got to me first.

"You look like hell," he said. "What have you done now?"

"And nice to see you, too," I said. "I'm fine, thank you very much. So good of you to be concerned."

The rest of the crew were a bit more appropriate in their greetings. My parents wanted me to go to the hospital, but I convinced them that it wasn't necessary.

"To tell you the truth, all I want to do is get out of this place," I said.

"I'll pack the bags," Andy said.

"Is that all right with you?" I asked Don Deutsch.

"I can't say as I blame you," he said. "But I'll need a statement from you before you leave."

"As long as I can shower and get into some dry clothes first. Oh, and I have to find my purse. It's somewhere on the trail."

"One of my men can look and bring it to the hotel," Don said.

"It's all right. If you want to come along, I can tell you where everything happened."

"Are you sure you're up to it?" my mother asked.

"I might as well get it over with."

"I'm coming, too," Edna said. She had her four-footed cane.

"We might as well all come, then," my father said, and we set off down the trail.

I was glad for the company. Going back into the woods alone held no attraction for me. When we got to the place I'd been sitting when Garth Elshaw found me, I pointed it out to Don Deutsch.

"Which way did he come from?" he asked.

"I'm not sure. I just heard a sound, turned around, and there he was."

"How did he seem?" Don asked

"Fine. He was saying how Morley used to like to come here. Then he told me about these birds Morley had seen last week or something. He said he'd show me. I thought he was lonely. I felt sorry for him."

I turned to Andy.

"Besides, I thought I could impress the hell out of you by bringing you back and showing you some fancy bird."

"So you went along the trail with him," Don said.

"Yeah. While we walked, we talked about Morley. I told him how sorry I was and so on, and we were speculating, or at least I thought we were speculating, on how and why he had killed Virna Wilton."

We had taken up our single-file parade again.

"I think I can find where we went to," I said. "And don't forget to keep your eyes peeled for my purse. Anyway, he mentioned something about the way Virna had died, something you had told me the public didn't know."

We came to a bend in the trail, and I paused. It seemed too soon to come to it, but I thought I recognized the place where he had gone to look for the birds. I stopped and pointed it out.

"Right down there," I said; then, to Andy, "There were American avocets."

I showed him where to look. He looked slightly guilty, but couldn't resist a peek. He came back grinning.

"Is it a new one for you?"

He nodded.

"Thanks."

"Can we get back to the part where my life was in peril, then?"

Don Deutsch and Hugh Grenfell were squatted down by the water, looking at the churned-up riverbank where we had fought. It made me feel a bit queasy.

"What you did took guts," Deutsch said.

"It wasn't courage, it was survival," I said.

The rest of the group caught up with us. My mother had my purse.

"I found it back there, beside the trail."

"Thank you," I said.

We all stood for a few moments looking at the river, then headed back up the path to the parking lot. We retrieved all our cars and retraced the route back to the hotel for the last time.

When we got there, the goodbyes began. Jack and Edna had been ready to leave when they heard about my adventure. Now they were anxious to get on their way to Edna's house in Watrous.

"Well, Kate, I'm glad you're still in one piece," she said. "I would have hated to lose my newest friend. I think we should appoint you an honorary All-American Girl."

"Not if I have to learn that stupid song," I said.

"Now, keep in touch. I've written down my address and phone number for you. Be sure and send me the article you write."

"I promise," I said.

"I'm just sorry I never actually got to see the Hall of Fame," she said. "It didn't seem right somehow. I guess I'm going to have to come back."

"It's worth the trip," I said.

"I'd hug you, but you're all over in mud, so I'll hug Andy instead."

She did.

Then it was Jack's turn.

"I'll give you my card," he said. "I still get up to Chicago from time to time. Maybe I'll make the trip next time the Titans are in town to play the White Sox. We can get together. Go listen to some jazz or something."

"That would be nice," I said. We embraced and then he and Andy shook hands.

"If you ever go on the road with Kate, it would be great to see you, too," Jack said.

"Maybe I will," Andy said. "Keep an eye on her."

"She could use it, if what went on here is any indication," Jack said.

"Can the helpless female talk?" I asked. "It seems to me I managed to look after myself just fine."

Jack turned to my parents.

"It was a pleasure to meet you both," he said. "You've been a great help to me over the past few days. If you're ever in Indiana, give me a call."

He shook my father's hand, and embraced my mother. She kept her arms at her sides but turned her cheek for his kiss, and I saw pain wash across her face in a brief, controlled, spasm. I had to look away, my throat tight.

"Good luck to you, Jack," she said. "It was nice to see you again after all these years."

"God bless," my father said. "Have a safe trip home."

Finally, Jack said goodbye to Don Deutsch.

"You'll let me know how things turn out?" he asked.

"Of course."

274

"Thanks for everything. I may want to come back for the trial, if I can."

"I'll let you know when it is," Deutsch said.

They drove off while we stood and waved.

"We'd better be getting a move on, too," my father said. "Merle and Stanley are expecting us in time for supper in Saskatoon."

Oh, God.

"I can't do it," I said. "I have to stay and give my statement, and to be frank, after the day I've had, I can't face another of Merle's meals. I'm sorry, Mum. Can you make excuses for me? Please?"

"Well, if you want to know the truth, I wish I could make an excuse myself," she said. "I don't know how my brother has survived all those years on her cooking."

"We'll drive down in the morning to catch our plane," I said. "So we'll say goodbye now."

"I'll just get the bags," my father said. Andy went with him.

I turned to Don Deutsch.

"To save time, I'll write out my statement on my laptop, then give it to you on diskette. That will save you having to transcribe it. I can bring it by the detachment to print out within the hour. Does that make sense?"

"Sure. I'll be there."

He left and I turned to my mother.

"Are you all right?" I asked.

"Certainly," she said, crisply.

"You looked a little choked up, before, saying goodbye to Jack."

She didn't say anything.

"Well, I hope everything works out," I said.

275

Andy and my father came out of the hotel with the bags and took them to the car. My mother and I followed.

"I'll call when we get home," I said, holding the passenger door open for her.

She got in, fastened her seat-belt, and rolled down the window.

"Thanks for coming," she said. "Both of you. I appreciated it. I just wish things hadn't turned out the way they did."

"Me too," I said.

As the car drove away, Andy and I waved.

"Alone at last," I said.

"I'll pack while you write your statement."

"And what then?"

"What's the fanciest hotel in Saskatoon?"

"I'm not sure. The Besserer, maybe. It's the grand old railway hotel, but I haven't been there in years."

"I'll research it while you shower," he said. "And book us the fanciest room in the joint. With hot and cold running room service."

"And a 'Do Not Disturb' sign for the door."

CHAPTER

42

It didn't take long for our life to get back to its normal, slightly chaotic, pace. Because Andy works days and I tend to work week nights during the season, we can go days without seeing one another awake, but we managed to overlap on an off-day to bury Elwy's ashes. We planted a lilac bush over him, so I'd remember him each spring, then Sally and T.C. joined us for a little wake. We drank champagne and told stories. Sally and I shed a small Presbyterian tear or two, but the evening was mostly telling stories about Elwy that made us laugh. It was a good way to say goodbye. T.C. told me about a friend with a litter of kittens, but I'm not ready to replace Elwy yet. I suspect Andy hopes I never will be, but I know from past experience that it won't take long for another cat to find me, one way or another.

I thought about my mother a lot, and about Jack. I was

tempted to confide in Andy, but managed to resist. Besides, I was too busy.

Work had turned into the kind of nightmare that only a pennant race can bring. The Titans had gone on a surprising winning streak, and were leading their division going into the stretch. Attendance was up, and callers to sports talk shows were whipping themselves into a frenzy about the possibility of a World Series in Toronto. This put extra pressure on everyone, not least the sports writers. Every game became important, and we were expected to take our magnifying glasses to every move the manager made or didn't make. As well, every executive at the paper had ideas about what our coverage should be.

Our little corner of the newspaper, the toy department, as it is called by the news side types, is usually a very pleasant place to work. Our editor, Jake Watson, is a genial and thoughtful man who actually believes that his writers are smart enough and responsible enough to recognize and follow through a good story, but with pennant fever sweeping both the city and the newsroom, he had to handle a lot of stupid questions and hare-brained suggestions from the higher-ups. This did not make him happy, and when Jake Watson isn't happy, neither is his staff.

I tried to keep my sense of humour, but it was stretched pretty thin. I almost wished the Titans would go on a losing streak so I could go back to working in pleasant obscurity again.

A couple of weeks after our return, I was sitting in the press box at the Titan Dome watching the home team beat the hapless Tigers when my direct line rang. I noted the walk that had just been issued to the leadoff batter in the bottom of the fifth into my score-book, then picked up the phone. It was Andy.

"Your mother just called," he said.

"On a Wednesday?"

"I know. I thought it might be important. I told her to call you there, but she didn't want to disturb you."

"Thanks. I'll call her back."

"What's happening in the game?"

"Titans winning big. Why don't you turn it on?"

"I've got better things to do with my life," he said.

"Well, pardon me. Anyway, it looks like it's going to be a long night."

The runner, Joe Kelsey, stole second.

"I won't wait up," he said.

"See you later."

Single to left, bobbled, Kelsey scored, runner to second on the error. I could do this job in my sleep. I made the symbolic notations in my score book, then dialled my parents' number, tucked the receiver into my shoulder and typed the scoring play into my computer while listening to the ringing signal.

"Mum, you called," I said, when she answered. "Is something wrong?"

"Oh, Kate, I didn't mean to disturb you. I just thought you should know."

"Know what? Nothing's wrong with Daddy, is it?"

Another walk and a wild pitch, moving the runners to second and third. The crowd cranked up the volume. I couldn't hear her answer.

"You're going to have to speak up, Mum. It's noisy here."

"I said, everything's all right." "It's just fine. I called because Jack Wilton phoned me yesterday."

"Oh?"

"It seems that when he was wrapping up Virna's estate, her lawyer gave him a letter she had left for him to read after her death."

"Oh."

Short fly ball out to left, runners hold.

"Yes, she told him the truth. And he called me."

"What was his reaction?"

"A combination of a lot of things, I guess. Surprise. Anger. Sadness. Excitement."

I realized that my mother was describing her own feelings.

"He didn't call me for several days," she continued. "I guess it took some getting used to."

Triple into the gap, two score. Pandemonium in the stands.

"Of course it did," I said. There was silence on the line.

"Mum?"

"I told your father last night."

"Oh, dear. How did he take it?"

"He was shocked, of course," she said. "But I think he's glad I told him."

"And how do you feel about all this?"

"Relieved, I think, finally."

"You're sure?"

"At first, I was very angry with Virna, too. She had no right to do that without warning me."

Walk.

"Well, Mum, maybe she meant to, out there at Battleford, and just didn't get to it. You're sure you and Daddy are all right?"

"Yes, he wants to speak with you in a minute."

"Have you told anyone else? What about Sheila?"

"No, I think I'll wait until I can tell her in person."

Passed ball, runner to second. Runner on third scores.

"Is it all right if I tell Andy?"

"If you feel you must."

"Not if you don't want me to. But we share most things."

"Use your own judgement, then."

Single, runner scores. Manager out of the dugout, pointing to his left arm. I put my pencil down. The PA system blared forth taunting music to welcome the new pitcher.

"I mustn't keep you from your work," she said.

"It's okay, Mum, we're in a pitching change."

"What's the score now?"

"Let's see. It's 9–0, and counting."

"That's nice. I'll get your father."

She put the phone down. I typed the scoring plays into the computer.

"Well, Kate, your mother continues to surprise me," he said, sounding a bit shaky, but also, what's the word? Brave, I guess.

"Oh, Daddy, are you all right?" I asked. I was getting strange looks in the press box.

"I'm all right, just a bit astonished."

"It was a long time ago," I said. "Before she even knew you. Don't be hard on her."

"Kate, I couldn't be as hard on her as she has been on herself for all of these years," he said. "I wish she had told me from the beginning. Then we could have been part of this young man's life all along."

"It's not too late now," I said.

"I know that. I spoke with him earlier this evening."

The warm-up was over. The batter stepped in.

"Are you sure you're okay, Daddy?"

"Don't worry about me."

First pitch. Ground ball. Double play. Inning over.

"I will, but not too much. I know you'll work it out. I've got to go now. Give Mum a hug for me. I love you both."

I hung up the phone and watched the grounds crew race onto the field with their rakes and brooms. I dug in my wallet for the card from the All-American All-Star Flower Shoppe in Fort Wayne. Jack had written his home number on the back of the card. I dialled it.

A woman answered, a woman with a strong, cheerful voice and an upward inflection at the end of her greeting. I asked for Jack.

"Can I tell him who's calling?"

"Tell him . . . " I paused.

"Tell him it's his sister, Kate," I said.